The
BEACH
ALIBI

The BEACH ALIBI

ALISON KENT

B
BRAVA

KENSINGTON PUBLISHING CORP.
http://www.kensingtonbooks.com

He who gains an indulgence is not, strictly speaking, absolved from the debt of punishment, but is given the means whereby he may pay it.
—Thomas Aquinas (1225–1274)
Summa Theologica

The
BEACH
ALIBI

One

He couldn't believe it.

He abso-fucking-lutely couldn't believe this was happening. Not here. Not now. No way.

He'd prepped for this mission for weeks. He knew every way into this building, every way out. Windows, elevators, ducts, doors, all of it.

He'd wallpapered his workstation with blueprints and surveillance photos, for fuck's sake.

How the hell could he have missed the goddamn camera hidden in the goddamn wall clock?

Kelly John Beach averted his head, stared at his black, rubber-soled shoes, at the pine green and navy leaf pattern in the executive suite's carpet beneath, and ordered himself to think, think.

Think!

The camera was new. The clock hadn't been here earlier tonight. He'd scanned this office an hour after the cleaning crew had left, doing an electronic sweep while in uniform as building security.

There had been nothing—*nothing*—on that wall other than the portrait of the company's founder. That didn't change the fact that now, at 2200, there was. Or the fact that the position he was in was more than compromising.

It was neck-in-the-noose illegal.

Proving that Marian Diamonds was working with the international crime syndicate Spectra IT to smuggle conflict diamonds out of Sierra Leone would hardly negate a breaking-and-entering or burglary charge.

Especially since explaining how he'd come to be in possession of such intel would put the Smithson Group at risk for exposure—exposure he couldn't let happen. That he *wouldn't* let happen . . . think, think.

Think!

The USB flash drive detailing the diamond shipments and subsequent buyers was now tucked safely into a pocket of the vest strapped to his chest, along with the rest of the tools of his highly suspect trade.

Getting out of here wasn't going to be a problem. He'd simply reverse the trip he'd made coming in. No, the trouble would come later.

Three minutes from now, he'd be ground level wearing street clothes. Give the cops another thirty, he'd be wearing handcuffs.

God-fucking-damn.

Sweat beaded on his forehead, rolled like Niagara down his spine. His eyeballs burned. His temples throbbed. His heart was a fist-sized red rubber ball clogging the base of his throat.

Plain and simple, he had to get to the SG-5 ops center without hitting the street. The only way to do that was the train at the Broad Street station. Then underground.

He hated going underground. He hated the dark. Hated the rats. Hated the stench of shit and decay and all the rotten crap he'd have to step in.

Fuck me blind. He growled, grumbled, snorted. Now he was really looking forward to the trip. But a man had to do what a man had to do, or so went the saying.

And so he did. Sucked it up, swallowed his own bullshit along with the red rubber ball, and walked out of the office like the fucking president of the U. S. of A.

"Slow it down, son. Slow it down." Hank Smithson gestured toward Kelly John with the stub end of a cigar tucked in the crook of his index finger. "You're not going to get this figured out by wearing a hole in the floor."

The older man could use his calming techniques all he wanted. Kelly John wasn't in any mood to be calmed or gentled or put out to pasture.

Not when it looked like what he was about to be was put down.

He paced the SG-5 ops center's huge horseshoe workstation from his own desk to Tripp Shaughnessey's and back. Again and again and again.

"Easy for you to say." Kelly John stopped, sniffed. Christ, but he smelled like a freakin' sewer. "You aren't the one who screwed up."

It was more than screwing up the mission and giving the upper hand to Spectra IT—the only ones with any reason to have Marian Diamonds bugged. The ones receiving the feed at the far end of the camera.

After what Tripp had gone through with the duo recently, that much was a given as far as Kelly John was concerned.

No, it was endangering the Smithson Group, jeopardizing everything Tripp, Julian and Christian, Mick and Eli and Harry had been working for, failing himself.

Failing Hank.

Hank crossed his arms over his chest and rocked back on his boot heels. "Kelly, you did your best."

His best hadn't been good enough. Not this time. A hell of a hard pill to swallow considering the reason Hank had picked him to join the Smithson Group in the first place.

"Spectra had to know I was coming." And he'd shoot

himself for that if it would help. "That's the only way the timing of that camera install makes sense."

"They were protecting their assets," Hank reminded him.

A reminder that pissed off Kelly John even further when he thought of the source of the organization's millions. "Yeah, well, now they've got video proving how insecure they really are. And how stupid I really am."

Hank moved, blocking Kelly John's path, commanding his attention. "We'll figure it out, son. We'll figure it out."

"What's to figure?"

At Tripp Shaughnessey's offhanded question, both men turned, Kelly John glaring down at his partner where Tripp sat on the floor in front of his desk. "What the hell's that supposed to mean?"

Tightening the wheels on his upended chair, Tripp shrugged. "You're the techno whiz. Make your own video. Prove you were elsewhere at the time. Show them they only think they know what they're seeing."

"An alibi," Hank said.

Intrigued, Kelly John started pacing again. "That might work."

"And we all know who makes the best alibi for a man, right?" Tripp asked.

Kelly John knew he wasn't going to like the answer. "Who?"

"A woman."

"Right. A woman." He scrubbed both hands over the sewer grit on his face. "Where the hell am I going to find a woman to back me up and not go mouthing off to all her girlfriends about what's going on?"

Hank shoved his cigar back into the corner of his mouth and grinned. "This one I've got covered."

Emma Webster had just packed up her Billy Bag satchel when the private line on her desk phone rang. It was six-thirty P.M., and she'd thought the office empty.

She'd gone down to the health club at five, had a quick salad at Brighton's after working out, then come back up-stairs to grab the novel she'd been reading at lunch before finally heading home.

Instead, she picked up the receiver on the third ring. It was Hank, and if he was still here and looking for her, her cell would be ringing next. "Emma Webster."

"Emma. Hank here."

"Hank. I thought you left hours ago."

"I was called out for a bit"—he cleared his throat—"and I'm afraid I've had an emergency of sorts dropped into my lap. I'm going to have to ask you for some over-time."

"I'll be right in." She took a deep breath and conjured up the image she'd checked in her cheval mirror before leaving her apartment this morning.

Not the image reflected back at her from the glass door to Brighton's ten minutes ago. The image of a woman who had spent the last hour sweating like a politician caught with a cigar and an intern.

Oh, well. An emergency was an emergency, even if she was wearing white cross trainers and slouch socks, hot pink Spandex shorts and sports bra, and a white pullover worthy of a wet T-shirt contest.

Not exactly an outfit conducive to professionalism. At least at this late hour, her boss should be alone.

He wasn't, of course, which was bad enough. Even worse was the six-foot-two, two-hundred-ten-pound, blue-eyed, black Irish reality of who was leaning on the edge of his desk.

One very sexy Kelly John Beach.

She placed her satchel on the thick carpeting just inside the door and crossed the expansive office, refusing to adjust her clothing or touch her hair, or give into any of the copi-ous nervous reactions to being seen at her absolute physical worst by the very man she most wanted to attract.

He was one of Hank's special Smithson Engineering project consultants. A group of men rarely seen around the office, but causing all tongues belonging to female employees to wag when walking through.

All tongues save for Emma's. In her position as Hank's assistant, wagging was unacceptable. She didn't speak out of turn. Ever. A well-known and well-documented fact that had helped land her this job.

She wondered for less time than it took her to reach Hank's desk if Kelly John was involved in the request for her overtime. The grave look the two men exchanged answered her question. She cringed, but only to herself, wishing like hell that she could step into this meeting on a more even footing.

But such was not to be when one wore hot pink Spandex. Even had she been wearing the pieces of her work wardrobe she'd had on earlier in the day, the balance would have leaned heavily in the male favor. As was too often the case.

"Sit, Emma, please," Hank requested once she'd reached his desk. She hesitated briefly, but it was enough to broadcast her discomfort at the disadvantage. He picked it up and added, "Let's all sit."

Emma took the seat closest to where she stood, Kelly John the one nearest the window. Hank dropped into his executive chair and braced his elbows on his desk, steepling his fingers as if the pious gesture would lessen the inappropriateness of the request.

Because the way both men seemed reluctant to speak to her or each other, or to meet her inquisitive gaze, she was certain inappropriate would barely cover what they wanted her to do.

She cleared her throat. "You mentioned overtime?"

"Overtime, yes. But this time it's more than my dad-blamed habit of procrastinating on paperwork." Hank paused, and color bloomed in the apples of his cheeks. "As a matter of fact, it's overtime giving you legal grounds to charge my sorry hide with sexual harassment."

"Oh, really," she said, blinking away the strangest sensation of being caught up in a fog-like dream. Even the words he'd spoken were weirdly surreal.

Hank Smithson had never, in the five years she'd worked for him, come close to crossing such a line.

At her side, Kelly John shifted to lean forward, bracing his forearms on his knees and lacing his fingers into one big fist. He hung his head, but she wasn't fooled for a minute.

He exuded the same tension she saw in the set of Hank's shoulders, the deeply creased furrows lining his brow.

The room, in fact, fairly crackled with the buzz of expectant anticipation. As if what hung in the air was a suggestive truth neither man wanted to address for fear of offending her beyond repair.

And suddenly she knew. She knew. The inappropriate request involved this man at her side.

The very man who all too frequently played a part in her dark-of-the-night fantasies. She wanted to shiver with the possibilities, but instead she tamped down a response that she feared would strip away her current advantage.

Especially as there was a little bird telling her she needed to hold onto all that she could.

"Well, now that you've warned me, I'll have to admit a rather prurient curiosity. This is hardly what I expected."

"And you shouldn't expect it. No woman ever should." Hank leaned back in his chair, laced his hands over the slightly rounded rise of his stomach. "And I suppose we could call off this whole kit and caboodle right now. Save us all what might turn out to be an uncomfortable circumstance."

At her side, Emma heard Kelly John blow out an audible breath. The sound of a scoff. A surrender. A pox on the situation that had brought them here.

She half expected him to push from the chair and walk out of the room, but he sat where he was and said nothing. Nothing to counter Hank's suggestion. No offer of another.

Her back straight to the point of being stiff, she crossed one leg over the other, laced her hands over her knees and said, "Actually, I'd like to hear everything."

"You sure?" Hank asked, giving her one last out.

She nodded. "You would hardly go so far out of character to suggest anything improper if you didn't feel it your best option."

That said, she waited, watching the glances that passed between the two men. The silent conversation—*Are you sure? I don't know. Is there any other way? None so simple.*—left her sitting literally on the edge of her seat, swinging her foot, nervously waiting for the balloon to pop.

It was Kelly John who pricked the fragile skin.

"I've gotten into trouble with one of my assignments. And the most convincing way for me to get out is to have you pose as my lover."

Two

He saw it in her eyes. What trouble could an engineering project consultant possibly be in that sex used as a cover would abrogate?

He should've seconded Hank's earlier motion that they call this off here and now.

The problem was that they had no time to implement a more intricate alibi. He might be the operative with the most technical expertise, but Tripp was the video genius.

The other man had spent all night and most of the day working his contacts and his equipment to pull this thing together.

It had to be a go tonight.

And Emma Webster was the final piece of the puzzle waiting to be snapped into place.

Her sea green eyes went wide like saucers. She blinked as if doing so would clear up what it was he had said. "You want me to pretend to be your lover?"

Her tone of voice was businesslike, a query made to an associate, rather than the incredulous hysteria he'd expected. The hysteria Hank had sworn wasn't a part of Emma's repertoire of reactions.

He nodded. "Yes, though it's more . . . complicated than that."

"Complicated?"

"More involved," Hank added. "Which is why I would never ask this of anyone else. And why asking it of you now makes me feel slimier than a snake's gut."

Kelly John sensed Emma's mind clicking like a hard drive stuck on a bad sector. She couldn't get beyond the scope of what she imagined they were asking her to do.

He wasn't having a much easier time stooping so god-damned low. It was time to spell it out. Make it clear for all parties involved.

He heaved out a sigh. "I got caught on tape last night in a place I had no business being."

"That's not entirely true, Kelly," Hank put in. "You were there because I sent you there."

"The trouble you're in happened on the job, then?" Emma asked.

"On a job I specifically asked him to do." Hank shifted forward in his chair. "None of this would be an issue if I hadn't handed him the assignment."

"None of this would be an issue if I hadn't been so careless." Kelly John refused to let the older man take the blame for a situation he never should have walked into.

Emma got to her feet then, held one arm tight to her middle, rubbed the fingers of the other hand to her forehead as she paced. Kelly John cast a look at Hank, who simply shook his head to say there was nothing to do here but wait.

The waiting was the problem. The wondering what Spectra was planning. The sweating it out to discover what he was in for. The speculating about whether Emma would help or knock him ass first to the floor.

She had every right. He wouldn't blame her a bit. He just

wished she would say something, would make up her mind. If she wasn't going to do this, he needed time to devise another—

"Would one of you verify something for me?" she interrupted his thoughts to ask. "This assignment you keep referring to. Does it having anything to do with Smithson Engineering? Or is this some off-the-record activity shared on a need-to-know basis? One I don't need to know?"

Hank broke the silence that followed with a deep chuckle. "Ah, Emma. You cut to the heart of the matter just like my Madelyn used to do."

One of Emma's arched brows went up. "I hope you gave her the answers she needed."

"She wouldn't have it any other way."

"Good. Then you'll understand that neither will I."

Kelly John's gaze shifted from one to the other until they reached what appeared to be a standoff. A situation that would not be remedied without more of a revelation than it would be safe for the older man to make.

His own existence was in jeopardy, sure, but he was only one gear in the much larger SG-5 machine. He was expendable. Hank was not.

And Emma learning the truth about Hank . . .

"I need to know how far I can trust you, Emma."

"Hank, wait." Kelly John surged to his feet at the same time Emma moved closer to say, "Trust shouldn't be an issue after all this time of working for you."

Her gaze came up to meet Kelly John's as she went on speaking to her boss. "Especially considering you have me handling the expense reports for your project consultants instead of sending them to accounting."

Her expression issued as much of a challenge as did her words. To be effectively involved, she would have to know the truth. Until this moment, however, Kelly John hadn't considered that knowing might also make her a formidable ally.

Hank was the last one to stand. "You're right. You've honored every word of your confidentiality agreement. If you hadn't, well—"

"If I hadn't," she interrupted, "I would have expected you to show me the door at the first breach."

Hank unlocked his gaze from Emma's, which was fiercely bold, turning to Kelly John. "This one's your woman, son. But only if you're comfortable bringing her in."

"If it were just my ass on the line, it would be one thing. But I've got to consider the others."

At that, Emma stepped in. "By others I'm assuming you mean Christian Bane, Tripp Shaughnessey, Julian Samms, Eli McKenzie, Mick Savin, and Harry van Zandt?"

Kelly John said nothing, acknowledged nothing, gave away no goddamn thing. His gut was on fire, his caution at this point not worth a plug nickel. Not if she knew what she seemed to.

How the hell could she know what she seemed to? How the fucking hell had she done it, rattled off the SG-5 names like she was running her finger down a roster?

He held her gaze fast until Hank cleared his throat. The sound broke the tension that had sweat rolling the length of Kelly John's backbone.

Emma glanced down and away, smoothed the hem of her T-shirt with the first show of nervousness he'd seen. Good. He wanted her nervous. Nervous meant she understood the significance of what she'd just done.

"I have never put those names together for anyone." Her voice was soft but firm, her words clear. "The connection is my own because of the work I do for Hank. Yes, I've had others on the office staff ask what I might know about any of you."

When she looked back up at him then, he thought for a

moment he wouldn't be able to breathe. Her eyes were that bright, her expression that intense. The set of her mouth that determined and grim.

For a sharp half second, he swore he was facing a member of the Smithson Group. One who understood the blood and the bond and the trust. Above all, the trust.

"But I do not talk out of turn," she went on to say. "Ever. Not even when faced with threats. If you don't believe me, pull up my record."

"Record?" he asked, his heart pounding with the fierceness of what he was feeling.

She nodded. "Before coming to work for Smithson, I was an investigative reporter. One of the cases I covered was a very high profile crime, and I spent three years researching and writing a book about it."

She took a deep breath before blurting out the rest. "The Justice Department later convened a grand jury, and filed charges when I refused to divulge a source. I was held in civil contempt as a recalcitrant witness.

"And I spent eight months behind bars."

She hated playing the jail time card; she really did. But she hated even more having doubts cast on her loyalty and integrity. And she had to admit surprise that Hank would be a party after all this time.

Still, she'd been curious enough about this request to pull out all stops, pleading her case.

And now here they were. Hank at her side, Kelly John behind, the three of them walking down the hallway of the twenty-fourth floor toward the DATA 2 TECH offices where Smithson Engineering's records were archived, databases generated, and Web sites served.

She knew there was no front office staff; when records were required to be pulled, an online order form was submitted, processed, and subsequently filled, whether for the legal or accounting departments, or for one of the engineers.

Which was why she couldn't imagine what business Hank Smithson or Kelly John Beach could possible have up here doing technical grunt work.

She fell in between the two men as they entered the reception area through the etched glass door, waiting with Kelly John while Hank punched the entry code into the panel granting interior access.

Through the small windows on either side, she was able to see the racks of servers. Not much of a view and certainly no hint of why they were here.

It was when the door opened and the three of them walked through that things got weird.

The boxlike room in which she found herself standing was suddenly lit by blinding overhead lights. The walls were bare, constructed of what appeared to be a soundproofing material no doubt intended as a security measure.

Why, she couldn't fathom, unless the server farm warehoused some sort of classified information beyond blueprints, schematics, and confidential records.

With her overactive imagination obviously in high gear, she squinted and watched Hank press his thumb to a scanning pad on the interior door.

Clicks and whirs and a vacuum release sounded as the door slid open, and *oh my* . . .

Her heart jumped wildly at the base of her throat. It was as if she'd walked onto a spy movie soundstage. Or the set of a television cop drama.

The server racks were nothing but a front; once inside, the room was a working office of sorts. Or not so much an office as what looked like a command center, a headquarters even. One secreted away from the public.

One currently occupied by three of the very men she'd named earlier for the two she was with.

She'd been right. Hank's project engineers had nothing to do with Smithson Engineering. They were anything but, what with their headsets and monitor banks and equipment she would need explained by James Bond's Q. Even then, she wasn't sure she would ever understand.

What she did understand were the guns holstered on the desktops.

She turned her gaze on Hank.

He snagged his unlit cigar stub from his mouth with two fingers and rocked back on his boot heels. "Welcome to the Smithson Group ops center."

Oliver Shore, Spectra IT's resident "professor," leaned back in the chair behind his desk in his Curaçao office, elbows braced on the padded arms, index fingers tapping his chin.

He stared at his visitor, who had arrived only moments before, having been whisked out of La Guardia on a private jet once the break-in had been discovered.

A break-in that left Oliver most disturbed.

"You were told to secure your office." The words fell like ice cubes. "To restrict access to the data detailing our arrangement."

Charles Marian wiped a hand over his brow to clear the perspiration. The response was not lost on Oliver, who kept his office at a chilly sixty-eight degrees.

The younger man, his ruddy complexion unnaturally pale, cleared his throat. "I don't know what happened. The cleaning crew came through. Security did their nightly check. The office shouldn't have been accessible."

"But it was. We have the infiltration on tape." Unfortunately, the infiltrator had not yet been identified.

That said, due to an encounter in a New York City sandwich shop a few weeks ago, Oliver had an idea as to the identity of the man—or at least the organization—with whom he was dealing, but would not take his suspicions to Spectra's higher ups until such had been confirmed.

Thanks to a recent acquisition allowing Spectra to crack the encryption, his team was currently running the tape through facial recognition software provided un-awares by the CIA. The confirmation should not be long in coming.

"Look," Charles said, still sweating, clammy, "I'm sorry. What else do you want me to say?"

Oliver got to his feet, planted his palms on his desktop's cool surface, and leaned forward, wishing any man but this one was his inside connection to Marian Diamonds. "I want you to say that you will instruct your uncle to reroute next week's shipment."

"He can't do that," Charles protested.

"He will do that. Unless he wants to find federal agents dragging him from his bed after they've seized the cargo. Or are you unaware of the penalties for smuggling conflict dia-monds?"

"No. I'm aware." Charles hung his head.

"And since your uncle is not a party to your agreement with our people in Africa, the penalty you face is even greater, am I not correct?"

Charles nodded, now pitched so far over his knees Oliver expected him to tumble unconscious to the floor. It was a shame how some men found themselves unable to handle deception.

A knock on the door brought Charles's head up and Oliver to his full height. He pushed his glasses into place and called out. "Yes?"

The door opened and Ezra Moore entered the room, his smile beacon bright against his black coffee complex-ion.

He wore his usual uniform of black T-shirt and pocketed cargo pants. A black bandana scooped his dreadlocks back from his face, exposing the strange diamond stud in the lobe of one ear.

When he spoke, his lilting island patois gave his announcement the rhythm of a song. "Oliver, it seems we won't be having a match."

"None at all?"

Ezra shook his head. "Nothing. The man does not seem to exist."

Oh, he existed all right. And Oliver was quite sure he knew where to find him. He smiled at the man standing just inside the doorway. "How do you feel about a quick trip to Manhattan?"

"Oliver, *mon*." Ezra shook his head. "You know how I feel about visiting the States."

"That I do, Ezra," Oliver said with a laugh. "That I do."

Emma Webster was the first outsider ever to visit Smithson Engineering's twenty-fourth floor. As far as the company's employees were concerned, Smithson leased the space to DATA 2 TECH.

The arrangement had worked well for quite a few years, and as far as Hank was concerned would continue to do so.

The tech firm was a legitimate subsidiary of the larger Smithson conglomerate, the corporate papers properly filed with state and federal agencies as required each year.

Hank wouldn't be risking the exposure now if not for Kelly's life being on the line.

Once Tripp had been made during the standoff at Brighton's a couple of months back, Hank had assigned Kelly the Marian Diamonds scenario.

Now, with the boy's cover compromised, it looked like Hank just might have to reel in this big fish himself.

He ushered Emma further into the room. "I believe you know Julian Samms and Tripp Shaughnessey." Both men nodded warily. Hank raised a brow and turned to the third operative. "This is Mick Savin. Mick, Emma Webster. My executive assistant."

Emma held out her right hand. Mick offered his left, his right arm still encased in a fiberglass cast while the bones in his forearm healed.

Emma gave him a sheepish smile. "I'm sorry. I didn't think—"

"No worries," he assured her, his curious gaze taking in Hank, as well.

Hank rested a palm on Mick's shoulder, nodded towards Julian, whose own arm was still strapped up in a sling. "Mick and Julian ran into a bit of gun trouble in Florida recently. They'll be fine."

Mick laughed. "Easy for you to say, mate. You're not the one who took the bloody bullet."

Hank gestured toward his bum hip. "Son, I'll put my shrapnel up against your bullet any day of the week."

At that, Mick laughed and headed deeper into the ops center.

Emma's gaze moved from one man to another until she'd taken in all five in the room, her attention lingering the longest on Kelly, a fact that did not escape Hank's notice.

He turned his back on his boys and spoke only to her. "These men work for me in a confidential capacity, as you suspected. If what they do is ever found out . . ."

He paused, gathered the truth of the matter close. "If what *I* have them doing is ever found out, every one of us'll be growing old behind bars. I wouldn't have brought you here if I'd thought doing so would compromise our work."

She crossed her arms over her chest, raised a brow. "Work, I'm assuming, you can't tell me about?"

He met the challenge of her gaze, once again reminded of

the reasons he'd hired her, of the choice he'd made to do so knowing that she wouldn't take his shit lying down and would dish him back the same.

"That's right," he said. "But even without being privy to the details, you can know this. That work's going to grind to a halt in a big hurry for one of my men without your help."

Her chin came up as, eyes sparkling, she nodded. "What exactly do you need me to do?"

"That's my girl, er, woman," Hank said, amending his statement at the death of the twinkle and the lift of Emma's brow. "Welcome to the SG-5 team."

Three

She couldn't believe it. She was going to be a spy. Or a spy apprentice, at least.

Not a bad assignment for a woman who'd been bitten by the sleuthing bug before being locked up and having the key to her career as an investigative reporter thrown away.

Emma Webster aka Mata Hari.

Silly maybe, but she liked the idea of going undercover and all that it implied. Especially considering with whom she would be engaging in all that hot spy action.

Unfortunately, there wouldn't be any action of any kind going on if she didn't get her act in gear. Kelly John would be here in twenty minutes. The plan was to have drinks, see an off-Broadway show, then go out for a late dinner.

Tripp Shaughnessey had apparently pulled strings and massaged contacts to set up this sting. Big Brother would be watching her and Kelly John perform at each stop.

Being on a need-to-know basis and all, she'd been told nothing more. Except that she held all the cards when it came to the intimate nature of each performance.

The thought made her sweat.

Never in her life had she faced such a long evening ahead—and all that went with it—with less than an hour to pull herself together. And it was the pulling herself together that was giving her hell.

Bathing and dressing with lightning speed, sweeping her hair back into an elegant ponytail, applying full makeup for the second time today . . . those tasks were nothing when compared with her assignment to pose as a woman in love with Kelly John Beach.

Especially when she was dying to get her hands on him.

Smoothing her hair before securing it with a sleek black barrette, she couldn't help but ponder how true it was that good things came to those with the patience to wait.

She'd been waiting to snag Kelly John's attention since the first time he'd walked into Hank's office after she'd been hired.

And, no. She wasn't so pathetic that she'd been pining for five years without acting on the desire. But his personnel records were sealed. She knew nothing about his marital status and hadn't the means or opportunity to ask.

He rarely put in an appearance in the Smithson Engineering offices, and her position as Hank's executive assistant dictated propriety and avoiding the office rumor mill.

Her interaction with Kelly John, in fact, was more a case of running across his name in the course of managing Hank's affairs and mooning over him privately.

No. Mooning wasn't quite right. Mooning implied she'd been sitting on her butt waiting to be noticed when in reality she rarely spent a weekend at home.

Even weeknights were taken up with the hundred-and-one-plus trivia tournaments and gallery showings and round-robin dinners with friends.

She did not moon. She lusted. Straight up. Plain and simple. Easy to understand when taken solely as a reaction.

His eyes were a stunning blue and fringed with incredibly dark lashes, lashes appearing even darker than his thick black hair and brows. His jaw was strong and well defined, as were his chin and his cheekbones.

But it was his mouth that got to her. He was rarely smiling when she saw him; he always seemed so focused, as if anything else would be less than his best, unacceptable, inferior, flawed.

It was that single imagined trait, that perceived confidence, that tied up the entire package with an irresistible bow. She so admired confident men.

Kelly John Beach did more for her underused female libido than any man she'd known. And that made no sense since she didn't know him at all.

Her reaction was one hundred percent physical—a shallow reality of which she was not particularly proud, though it did produce a twinge of sympathy for the male of the species so often accused of the same.

There was just something about a big man, one who wasn't bulked up or muscle-bound but was perfectly proportioned from head to toe in size extra large.

Kelly John stood at least six foot two, meaning tonight she got to wear her highest heels without fear of looking over when walking beside him and seeing the top of his head.

A small consideration, but she enjoyed being with a man who made her feel feminine and small. Not that she was an Amazon, but she was definitely taller than the national average.

She turned this way, turned that, checking her reflection in her bedroom's cheval mirror. Her hair worked, her heels worked. Her little black dress worked, too.

Now to not fall apart while waiting for Kelly John to get here. Or to stumble all over herself once he arrived.

As if waiting for her to acknowledge the very real possibility of such, a knock on the door sounded. Her heart jumped from the center of her chest to the base of her throat before she could turn.

Still facing the mirror, she watched the rise of color from her neckline to her chin where it settled into her cheeks.

The flush was definitely that of a woman anticipating her lover. Since that was exactly the role she was playing, she took the reaction as a very good sign.

It was the purely sexual tautness low in her belly that she wasn't quite so sure of.

The only way this scraping-the-bottom-of-the-barrel plan would work was if he got his hands on her now.

He'd decided that on the cab ride over, knowing he'd have to make it fast. They had little time to spare and needed to be on their way.

But if he got his hands on her now, she'd know what to expect later, and her reaction wouldn't be one of a condemned woman facing a firing squad.

Kelly John knocked a second time, waiting for Emma to make up her mind, to decide whether his ass was worth saving.

Because for all her spouting off in Hank's office about her loyalty to her boss, she had no idea what she was getting herself into.

That by the end of tonight, her life might very well be strung up next to his on the line.

The door opened. She smiled, standing there looking nothing like the woman he knew from the office. Not that he knew her well—or knew her at all—but he'd seen her. He'd noticed her.

He'd just never expected . . . this.

Her legs started with incredibly high heels and disappeared beneath the midthigh hem of a black dress he'd have to ruck up to her waist to get under.

The thought gave him pause . . . and an electrical buzz over the skin cupped tight to his balls.

He nodded, keeping his gaze on her face and away from her deeply scooped neckline and the gorgeously plump curves of her tits. "May I come in?"

"Sure." She took a step back. "I thought you might be in a hurry. I'm ready to go."

He followed her inside, pushed the door closed behind him, swore not to think about the perfect fit of his cock and her cleavage. "One thing I'd like to do before we go."

"Okay," she said slowly, looking up at him with her eyes wide and her smile not quite so. "What is it? Can I help?"

He was the one who smiled then, who took a step closer, who shook his head when she started to back away. "You can help by standing still."

"Okay," she said again, gesturing with one hand. "And what else?"

He took hold of her hand, brought it to his chest, held it there so she could feel the desperate beat of his heart. "You can let me kiss you. And you can kiss me back."

"You want to kiss me?" she asked, spreading her fingers wide there, his sternum beneath her palm.

She flexed her fingers once, twice, her gaze caught by the movement as if seeing his bare skin instead of his black suit coat and gray blue dress shirt sans tie.

When he didn't answer immediately—or at all—she raised her gaze and asked him again with her eyes. *You want to kiss me?* And suddenly he realized there was nothing he wanted more.

A want that caught him like a hard knock to the jaw because it seemed so right for all the wrong reasons.

"Yeah," he said softly, covering her hand with his, "I do. We get this out of the way now, things will be less awkward later."

It took her a minute, but she finally nodded. And then she wet her lips. "You're probably right. Nerves don't make for a very convincing argument."

"Yeah. My thinking, too." His heart tripped faster; the way she caught her lower lip between her teeth was a dead giveaway that she'd noticed.

"So," she began, smoothing back her hair with her free palm. "Here? Now?"

Her voice was breathless. That much helped, the fact that what they were doing wasn't sitting any easier with her. He brought his hand up to cup her face, hoping she understood the reality of what he was facing.

And that she wasn't two steps away from backing out.

He nodded, gave her a tight smile. "Here and now works just fine."

She slid both hands up his chest to his neck, cradled his nape first, then the base of his skull, and lifted her face, lips parted, eyes sharp as if taking him in like she would the rules to an exam.

Or better yet. Like a freak on display behind bars.

No, he thought, shaking his head. He wasn't going there, couldn't afford to go there, not now. Not with Emma's mouth inches away, his balls buzzing, and his life worth whatever they made of this night.

He lowered his head, covered her mouth, took full advantage of her lips, which were yielding and accepting and so very hot when she kissed him back.

She slipped her tongue along his, played with his, tempted his, withdrew and seduced him into her mouth. Wet, wild, and wow, he mused, that same tingling sensation wrapping tight fingers around the base of his cock.

This was no kiss for show, no role for which she was practicing, no test drive of the goods. This was the real deal; he turned her and backed her into the door, held her by the waist, and ground his mouth hard against her.

She whimpered, continued to kiss him while pulling him closer. She threaded the fingers of one hand into his hair, used her palm in the small of his back to urge him to step into her body.

He did, spreading his legs open on either side of hers, dipping his hips so that there was no mistaking what it was pressed like a piston into her belly.

When she wiggled against him, he reacted like any sane man and slid his hands from her waist up her ribcage to the sides of her breasts.

He'd been right. She wasn't wearing a bra. And she would fit him like a glove.

He palmed her nipples until they popped like gumdrops. He wanted a taste, wasn't sure he could tear his mouth free, didn't know if this was the time or the place to take things so far with the night that stretched ahead.

The thought returned him to the moment and the reason he was here. It wasn't about getting laid, even if the distraction of sex did a bang-up job of taking his mind off the threat to his life.

A fact that surprised him because he'd never been ruled by his dick. Though he was certain that would have been true in this case, had the woman in his arms been anyone but Emma.

He gentled the kiss, moved his hands to her shoulders, eased his mouth away. She appeared shell-shocked, much as he felt. A situation that reinforced for him that he'd been right to suggest they get this first strike out of the way.

He smiled, felt her answering one like a lead pipe to the back of his knees. Stumbling through the rest of the night wouldn't be so bad, he supposed. He'd look the pussy-whipped part he was playing.

"Well," she finally said, stepping around him and out of his space, "I suppose that went well."

He nodded. Well was weak compared to what he'd been thinking. "We should go. The cab's waiting."

"Sure. Let me fix my lipstick, grab my bag, and I'm ready."

Gripping the doorknob as if nothing else in the room existed, he decided it was a good thing one of them was.

Four

The cab ride over had been too quiet. The bar now was way too loud. Emma couldn't decide which was better.

Being able to hear nothing but her own thoughts because she couldn't raise her voice above the crowd, or because the man at her side hadn't said a word since nearly kissing her out of her panties.

Okay. That wasn't quite true. They'd talked. Small talk. Surface talk. Nothing talk. Smithson Engineering's paid parking and 401K plan. The weather. The depiction of the city on television in the *CSI* and *Law & Order* shows.

Stuff she supposed was first date material. But not anything to do with the reason they were here.

She lifted her glass, sipped at the Vodka Collins, needing to keep a clear head, though getting a good buzz would go a whole lot farther in the breaking down of inhibitions department.

Not that she'd been much the Catholic school girl earlier when faced with Kelly John's hands and mouth and impressively packaged lower body.

Oh, the lashes Sister Agatha would've administered had she been witness to the scene. Emma stirred her drink with her straw and laughed softly, figuring more than the backs of her thighs would've been switched black and blue.

"Something funny?" Kelly John asked, taking her by the elbow and guiding her away from the small cluster table where they'd been standing to an equally small corner booth that had just come available.

She slid into the half circle seat padded in hot aqua and hotter pink, feeling much like she'd dropped into a gumball machine as colored lights strobed over head. Kelly John slid in at her side, cornering her, though not threateningly, with the bulk of his body.

She waited for a shiver to pass before speaking, crossed her legs so that the toe of her shoe caught the fabric of his pants leg. "I was wondering how many lashes Sister Agatha would have doled out had she caught one of her girls in junior health class ever kissing a boy like that."

She didn't have to explain the *that*. He got it. "Is that where you learned, then? In Catholic school?"

"To kiss?" she asked, glad they'd moved. It was easier to hear over here. Easier to focus solely on him and tune out the unwanted noise.

He shook his head, lifted his rocks glass, glanced up briefly as he did. "To kiss like *that*."

She watched him suck back the Seven and Seven, caught speechless by the idea that the kiss had been more for him, as well. More than the usual. More than he'd expected.

Just . . . more.

"Uh, no. And to be honest"—she lowered her eyes, toyed with the rim of her glass—"I'm not sure I've ever experienced a kiss like that before."

Kelly John stretched his arm along the seat back and leaned forward, his fingers plucking at strands of her ponytail. She glanced up, meeting his gaze, dark and heavy-lidded and echoing with man's wicked appreciation of women.

When he spoke, his voice was low, husky. Raw. "Smile at me, Emma."

She did, and even she knew the lift of her lips wasn't true but false with nerves and anticipation. Canting her head flirtatiously, she tried again, whispering, "Sorry. I'm not so good with this acting thing."

His fingers moved from her hair to stroke the skin of her nape, the length of her neck beneath her ear, the exposed line of her collarbone. "Then don't act. Be as real as you were when you kissed me."

A tall order. She had no idea where *that* real had come from. And searching his eyes to find it brought the tightness back to her tummy, caused dampness to blossom between her legs as if sex was the obvious endgame.

And if it were?

The thought of the erection he'd pressed to her earlier, the thought of him sliding slowly, deeply, into her body produced the sort of smile he'd been waiting for, one that left her breathless with all she saw in his eyes.

"Is that better?" she asked, her voice as raspy as his.

He moved in closer, his upper body pressing her back into the booth, his mouth hovering along the edge of hers, his breath warm on her skin. She thought she might melt into butter there in the seat. He was amazingly hot.

Oh, how short had her fantasies fallen.

"There's a camera in the corner. In the light fixture." He lifted her chin with two fingers, caught the corner of her lips with his. "Keep your eyes on me, and we'll have what we need in no time."

What she needed was a cold shower or a stiffer drink or Kelly John between her legs. "You want I should kiss you back?"

Her words hovered over his skin like a mirage, like heat waves shimmering above asphalt. She felt them, and she waited. And waited, breathing him in, her nipples tightening, her sex swelling, wanting, aching.

Unbelievable, this desire for this man she hardly knew,

this man who had shown her what she'd been missing with a kiss she hadn't known existed.

When he nodded, she turned her face ever so slightly and tasted his lips with the tip of her tongue. He opened his mouth, but only enough for her kiss to fit, for her tongue to touch the cool edge of his teeth, for her mouth to tremble with wanting him.

The contact was simpler than their first time but no less intense. The simplicity introduced a new intimacy, a secret, a bond, until Emma felt she and Kelly John were breathing the same air, sharing heartbeats, waiting for the other to be the first to move away.

She didn't want to move anywhere that took her out of his reach. What she wanted was to get into his lap, beneath his clothing, under his skin the way he'd worked his way down to the surface of what made her tick.

She caught his lower lip between hers, ran her hand over the hard muscles of his thigh, wishing they had never left her apartment, that they'd tumbled into bed there instead of coming here to perform for a camera. . . .

She squeezed his leg, loving the way the muscle barely yielded, and reluctantly released his most kissable mouth. She'd been caught up in a fantasy of hot sex with a hot man when this encounter had nothing to do with her orgasms and everything to do with keeping him alive.

She did cup his face, brush his hair back over his ear. "You're an amazing kisser."

"Ditto," he said gruffly, taking hold of her hand and pressing his lips to the center of her palm. When he looked up into her eyes, he did so from beneath those long, dark, paintbrush lashes. "What else did you learn in Catholic school?"

She grinned without prompting. "You can't begin to imagine."

"Try me," he said, releasing her hand and reaching for his drink.

She did the same. "Okay, then. Cleanliness is next to god-liness. Nuns possess an otherworldly ability to detect nico-tine."

His responding chuckle encouraged her to continue. "Let's see. Rosary beads are not designed as accessories so forget trying to coordinate them to your uniform. And, no matter how much we might wish it so, Latin will never die."

His elbow propped on the table, his hand holding his glass, he shook his head. "So, basically, Billy Joel got it all wrong."

"Yes, exactly. We were all much more interested in sin-ners than saints."

"And now?"

"I think I've managed to find a nice balance and done so"— she held up one finger—"without splitting my personality."

He didn't respond except to down the rest of his drink in one gulp, signal to the passing server for another. While waiting, he reached for the hand she'd lowered to the table, stroking his thumb over the backs of her fingers.

The slow lazy motion no doubt looked good on camera, but no camera she knew of could capture the tension swathing their tiny corner of the bar. What the hell had she said?

Sinners and saints and split personalities. Which one of the three had set him off?

Would he have given up more of his anger than revealed by the tic at his temple if there hadn't been a camera in the room? And what about that anger? Was it self-directed or, as she feared, aimed at her for whatever it was she had said?

Less than an hour into this assignment and she was al-ready screwing things up. She turned over her hand to lace their fingers together. "I'm sorry. I said something wrong. I'm not sure what it was."

He shook his head, still not looking at her. "It's not you. It's—"

"—me. It is me," she insisted, because she hated that

lame excuse more than she hated anything. "What did I say? I need to know so I won't say it again. I don't want to mess this up for you."

She reached up with her free hand to stroke his cheek, to brush back the hair over his ear as a lover might do. Part of the caress was the act.

But another part, a larger part, was the pleasure she got from the contact of her skin to his. A pleasure that seemed so simple, yet one so rich with meaning, one she hoped might convince him of her sincerity, her determination to do this thing right.

It was what came beyond tonight that excited her. And terrified her. After tonight, they wouldn't be on display in front of an unknown audience. They would be two people with an intimate history, and she didn't want to tell him good-bye.

Not without more of a reason than this assignment coming to an end. "Kelly?"

His gaze rose; he turned his face into the cup of her palm. "Split personalities. I feel like that defines my life. That being myself got left behind when I went to work for Hank."

She lowered her free hand to their joined ones on the table, holding his between both of hers. "You do this a lot, then? Pretend to be someone you're not? Or at least pretend to be in a situation that's, uh, not quite one hundred percent real?"

"You don't think this one is real?"

She considered him carefully. "Well, it's not, is it? At least this part. The you and I part? We're not involved the way it would obviously seem to anyone walking by."

Or anyone viewing a tape later, she almost added, stopping because that was a scenario that made this situation very real for him.

He was acting with her, yes. But that was it. That was all. The rest was one hundred percent genuine.

And when the curtain came down, only then would he know if the role had saved his life.

She didn't want to mess things up for him; that's what she'd said.

She hadn't said she wanted to do right by Hank or perform well because she took pride in her job. She hadn't said she wanted to be sure her involvement didn't jeopardize her own life.

She'd said she wanted to do this right for him, because of him.

What he couldn't figure was why.

Standing near the back hallway and waiting while Emma did her thing in the rest room, Kelly John thought back over the evening so far, amazed how easy she was to be with, how well she played her part.

How much he wished this was real and not a scenario involving Spectra IT. Those just never did go down well. Even should everything turn out like a peach, parading Emma for the crime syndicate's radar was going to haunt him forever.

Considering he was already haunted by what had gone down in Nicaragua, he doubted he'd be losing more sleep than he normally did.

Or maybe he would, he mused, pushing off the wall on which he was leaning as Emma came into view, and swallowing like a man whose thirst would never be quenched.

Oh, yeah. Sleep would be lost. For reasons having nothing to do with Spectra and everything to do with her very long legs.

five

They hoofed it the six blocks to the theater. Once outside the club, Kelly John had started to hail a cab. Emma had stopped him. They had time, she said. The evening was breezy, her shoes quite comfortable, and she'd enjoy the walk.

Had she said she didn't want to be cooped up with him in close quarters, she couldn't have been more clear.

Still, she walked at his side. Close to his side. Touching the hem of his jacket, twining her fingers with his. Brushing arms. Dropping her head to his shoulder for a moment while she laughed.

"You sure your feet aren't killing you?" he asked, because he couldn't imagine walking more than a meter in the shoes she had on.

She laughed again. The sound was musical, a storm of notes that whirled around him, tightened up and touched down deep in his gut. "I wouldn't have suggested we walk if I thought I couldn't make it."

"Yeah, but there's a difference between making it and making it with nothing left but two bloody stumps." He glanced down at her feet. Slender and sexy and attached to the end of legs that made him drool like a Neanderthal. "Those heels look like wicked-ass finishing nails."

"Then you'll just have to trust me that there's plenty of padding between the shoe's heel and mine. I'm not feeling a thing."

He shrugged, stuffed his hands in his pants pockets. "If you say so."

"What?" She sidestepped enough to look over. "You don't trust me?"

Trust. The crux of the matter. Trusting Hank that this scheme would work. Trusting her not to spill the beans. Trusting himself not to make another one of the monumental mistakes he'd become so proficient at making.

Still, he said, "I wouldn't be here if I didn't."

She was quiet for several moments, finally moving nearer and hooking her arm through his. "Do you think anyone is watching us now?"

"If I say no, are you going to let go?"

"Do you want me to let go?"

He studied the crowd walking around them, sought out couples holding hands or strolling with arms joined, noticed others occupying adjacent space with zero connection, ignoring one another, zoned out rather than tuned in.

"No. I want you to stay right here," he said, uncertain why having her close seemed to matter, if it was a look he was going for or a feeling he craved.

He went so far, in fact, as to cover her hand with his, there where it rested in the crook of his arm. Her fingers were slender, long and cool, and he imagined the feel of them between his legs, cupping his balls, ringing his cock.

And then he quit imagining all of that because they still had four blocks to go.

Emma managed in the next second to make things worse by cuddling up even closer, pressing the plump side of her breast to his biceps. "This is rather ridiculous to ask at such a late date, and I'm not sure it would change anything any-way or if it matters, but are you seeing anyone?"

He was wishing he was seeing her naked, his cock buried between her tits. His voice rattled when he finally found it, and he swore if his mind didn't rise from the gutter, he was going to kick his own ass. "My career's not exactly con-ducive to dating."

She considered that for a moment, came back with, "Because of that thing about not being able to be yourself?"

That wasn't it as much as not trusting himself. "That, yeah. And if I didn't make it home, there would be too many ques-tions. And no one around to answer them."

Again she fell silent, weighing what he'd said. She had to be the most thoughtful woman he'd met in awhile, always thinking before speaking, always saying the right thing.

He could see why Hank had hired her. Why Hank hadn't hesitated bringing her onto the team. Why he himself couldn't think beyond the idea of bedding her.

"So," she was saying, "the girlfriends you have had haven't known what it is you do."

"I don't have girlfriends. I have . . ." *Shit.*

How was he supposed to explain that one without sounding like a pig? To tell her he had sex, not relation-ships, and that he never gave the women involved his real name?

"Sex, right?" she asked, and he nodded.

Perceptive again, though with the way he'd jolted to a halt, the answer was fairly obvious. At least she hadn't let go of his arm, even if her steps had slowed.

He only hesitated explaining because of how compli-cated their situation was. And because he didn't want her to think that when they fell into bed—*when, not if*—it would have anything to do with this mission.

Of that much he was certain. That they would fall into bed, that they would enjoy the hell out of each other, that they would go their separate ways once all was said and done.

She swatted at a buzzing fly. "Does that bother you? That you don't have anyone to share your life with?"

"I share my life with my team." He banked on them, knew they'd tell him when was screwing up and being a shit since he obviously needed someone to.

A car horn blasted, tires screeched. Kelly John gathered up what he needed to say next. "But if you're asking about not having a relationship with a woman, then no. It's a sacrifice that I rarely give a second thought."

"You called it a sacrifice."

"Yeah, so?" He shrugged out of his jacket, hooked it over his shoulder, giving her no choice but to release his arm.

"Well," she said, gesturing with her near hand, the one with which she'd been holding him, "then it's something you wouldn't have given up had you not chosen this career."

He snorted as they stopped for a traffic light. "There wasn't a whole lot of choosing involved in my coming to work for Hank."

She waited until they'd crossed the intersection before responding. And then her tone made it clear that she thought he was dissing the boss.

"I don't see how he could force you to do anything you didn't want to," she said. "Especially when it puts your life in danger. That's just not who Hank is."

Kelly John knew exactly who Hank Smithson was, as did every one of the Smithson Group operatives.

Simplifying it so she would understand, however, might be more than he could manage with his life on the line, his debt to Hank private, his record lately for big time fuck-ups glaring in bloody neon.

"That's not what I meant." If she still thought him an engineer, this would be harder to work his way around.

But with Hank's blessing and trust and being strung up as he was by the balls . . . "The choice I was talking about was one I had to make, not one forced on me by Hank."

"Oh," she said, and then she fell silent. They continued to walk side by side, though she seemed more interested in holding her purse than holding onto him.

And that just wouldn't do.

Not when he needed her all over him for cover, wanted her all over him because he just did. He moved toward her, hooked his arm around her neck and pulled her close.

She didn't argue; she even smiled. He liked both and found himself relaxing in response. "Sounded earlier in the office like you've made a few tough choices of your own."

The sound she made was nothing less than a snort. "Not exactly a time in my life I look back on fondly. It's rather weak in the pleasant memories department."

Yeah. He knew about unpleasant memories. He also figured comparing war stories wouldn't make for good first date fodder. Especially considering the tone of this date.

Nothing like the mental picture of prison bars to kill the sexed-up mood.

Still, he wasn't ready to let it go. She intrigued him, this woman who'd been through what she had, who now knew what she knew about who she was working for, who hadn't run screaming into the night with the discovery of that truth.

She was staring down the same gun barrel he was. A brave one, his alibi Emma Webster, and he drew her body close. "Not pleasant, no. But you stood up for your beliefs."

Another snort, a tilt of her head toward his. "And without even a book to show for it."

"Have you thought about writing about what you went through?"

She shook her head. "I've had publishers come calling."

"And?"

"I thought about it, but writing it would mean reliving it, and I'm not a big fan of self-abuse."

"Might work as therapy."

"Sure, if I were still needing to work through it. I pretty much did that at the time."

A lot healthier way of dealing than he'd managed, but then he'd been facing a death penalty before Hank made all records of his charges disappear.

"Can I admit something?" she asked as they turned at the next block and the theater marquee came into view.

"Sure."

"I'm not thrilled with the idea that I might wind up back there for doing this."

"That's not a worry. Nothing you're doing is illegal." He didn't tell her how much worse it might be. That being behind bars could be a fate much preferable to falling into the hands of Spectra IT.

"If you're sure."

He nodded, brought them to a stop at the end of the queue to go in. "I am. If anything's off kilter, it'll be what Tripp and I do with the tape."

"Ah, so, it's just questionable company I'm keeping?"

She asked it with enough of a tease to her voice that he couldn't help but glance over. Her eyes were sparkling, as were her cheekbones, as if dusted with a glittery powder. She looked like magic, and he liked it a lot.

Liked it enough that he kissed her. He used the hook of his elbow around her neck to pull her close, and he kissed her.

She opened her mouth, cupped the back of his head, and kissed him back right there in front of God and the theater crowd.

Her tongue nimbly teased and stroked and played with his. Her lips sucked lightly; her teeth nipped gently. All he wanted to do was fuck the foreplay and take her to the down-and-dirty ground.

But he didn't. He teased and stroked and played right back until his balls protested and the slit in the tip of his cock opened and wept.

It was then that he eased back, leaving her with one lingering kiss, then stepping away and gulping enough air to float a battleship.

She pressed her lips together, wet them with her tongue as if tasting him. And he swore there wasn't a person in line deaf to his groan. The woman was going to kill him, kill him where he stood.

"That wasn't for any camera, was it?" she asked breathlessly, the color high in her cheeks, the crowd around them applauding as she ran her thumb beneath his mouth to wipe away her lip color.

"Uh-uh." He shrugged back into his jacket, adjusted the front hem accordingly. "That was all for me."

She blew out a sigh that spoke volumes. She was no less affected, no less aroused. No less aware of where they were headed, this mission be damned.

"Okay, then." She opened her tiny purse for a mirror and her lipstick. "Just wanted to be clear on that."

"And are you?"

"Oh, yeah," she said, nodding. Once finished repairing her makeup, she tucked the items back into her purse and looked over. "Considering neither one of us will be acting when the time comes, I'd say our performance should be Oscar caliber."

For a very long tense moment, a very hot moment, a moment during which sweat pooled at the base of his spine and his balls twitched and burned, he waited.

Then he found his voice and said, "At intermission, we'll hang back. There's a hallway the servers and staff use."

"And that's where the camera is."

"The main one we'll be using, yeah."

She pulled in a deep breath, lifted her chin, smoothed a hand back over her hair. "Then I guess there's only one thing left to say."

"What's that?" he asked.

She answered with a siren's smile. "Break a leg."

The satellite phone in Ezra Moore's pocket buzzed against his thigh like the rattle on the long end of a snake. It would be Oliver calling to see that he'd disembarked safely, that he remained on schedule after the private jet's touch-down.

Ezra was both. Safe and on schedule. He wasn't, however, wanting to speak to the other man. Not yet. Oliver wouldn't be pleased to be relegated to Ezra's timetable, but Ezra had long ago decided he would control his own destiny, answering therefore to no man.

Not even to Oliver Shore, who was looking to one day hold the reins of Spectra IT. An event that would never come to pass while Ezra remained alive.

He slung his pack over his shoulder and made his way across the tarmac toward the car assigned to the Spectra hangar. It would be a short ride to the main terminal. Once there, he would switch to a taxi for the trip to the city.

Ah, but he loved the city. The noise and the lights and the people. Most especially the people. How easy it was to blend in, to do his work, to avoid detection, to get away with every deception he needed to.

The deceptions had become remarkably easy, these identities he assumed, the skins he wore like costumes. He stalked and he prowled and he moved in for the kill, leaving behind no more than a carcass, picking his teeth with the bones.

He embraced situations capable of castrating lesser men. It was where he found his power and his pride. And where the distinction was made between hunter and hunted, master and slave.

He'd been a lesser man once, subject to others who thought only of immediacy, of the instant gratification to be had with the deployment of cluster bombs and bunker busters.

Others who had lost their sight and their way, for whom long range was only accomplished with missiles, who acted in the heat of the moment, seeking revenge, retaliation.

Now those same men were subject to him because he understood the value, the necessity, the beauty of seeing the world through the glass of a crystal ball. Through tea leaves spelling out the power inherent to the individual. Through a palm delineating the road a man was called to travel.

All figuratively speaking, of course—though his great-grand-mère, still living on the island of San Torisco, would tell him that nothing was anything unless it was literal. And that he knew damn well that he had inherited her sight.

Perhaps he had. Perhaps this was the reason he was so clear on what it was he had to do. Who he had to save.

Who he had to kill.

Six

They were headed straight into bed.

Well, maybe not straight, because they did have the rest of this show and then dinner to get through, but after that . . . Emma trembled in her seat, as much from the anticipation as the feel of Kelly John's tickling fingers.

They sat in the rear of the theater; she could see the security cameras in both of the front corners far above the stage. She'd attended how many shows here, and never before noticed the pinpoints of red light?

These weren't the cameras that mattered, however. Those were in the hallway and would be the ones to capture their intimate performance—assuming she didn't succumb to a case of the vapors before the curtain was lowered for intermission.

Kelly John sat leaning toward her, his arm on the back of her seat, his hand draped over her shoulder, his fingers toying with the skin exposed by her low-cut neckline. He brushed the area beneath her ear, and she shivered anew.

She'd totally lost track of the play. *The Importance Of Being Earnest* had, however, taken on a personal interpretation, one steeped in the warmth of Kelly John's breath where it stirred stray strands of her hair.

She glanced over in the dark, looked up at his profile from beneath lowered lashes. His jaw was set, a sexy shadow of beard adding another layer of intensity to his focus. And he was focused, though she knew his attention was not on the show.

It was as if he was biding his time and no more. Waiting for the hands of the ticking clock to sweep their way around. For the crowd to exit, to mingle, to drink and to laugh, to engage in conversation, the tone of which would signal their reaction to the play.

And then the real show would begin. The show for which she and Kelly had really come.

As if reading her thoughts, he tilted his head, his eyes cutting away from the stage to find hers, study hers, look into hers so fiercely that her throat closed up tight.

The whites of his eyes were bright, his pupils dark, the rings of his irises iridescent. Her stomach fluttered; she thought of lying beneath him, his body buried deep within hers, looking up into those very same eyes.

She squeezed her thighs together, slipped her closest hand into his lap, and absorbed his body's heat with her palm. Her skin burned. Her stomach twisted and turned and knotted tautly. She was never going to make it through the night.

His gaze dropped to her mouth. She wanted to lick her lips, to part them, to tempt his kiss, but she did nothing except watch his face and wait.

She wanted to know what he was thinking, if his imagination had traveled in the same direction as hers. If he thought of where he wanted to feel her lips, her tongue, the heat of her mouth.

In the end, she was the one who groaned, and he was the one who raised his gaze slowly and smiled. The look he gave her then said more than a thousand words.

He was thinking every heated thing she was and more. A

more that she was certain existed outside of everything she knew. A more that she wanted him to show her.

And when the curtain rose for the second time tonight, he would.

"Are you sure you won't miss not seeing the rest of the show?" Emma stood in the theater lobby, a glass of white wine in one hand, her beaded bag in the other, that arm hugging her middle tight.

She pressed her back to the wall beside the bar as the crowd began its slow crushing return to the auditorium. Her nerves were strung high to the point of near giddiness, a state that she couldn't see as being conducive to the staged seduction that was tonight's main act.

Kelly John stared as if she'd spoken using the mouth of her second head. "Are you freakin' nuts? I couldn't even tell you what the hell's going on if I wanted to."

She laughed, nearly sputtering her last drink of wine. "Bored or distracted or both?"

He'd been standing with his back to the bar, his weight in the shoulder he'd braced on the wall. But now he moved in closer, angling his body across hers and dipping his head.

His lips hovered above hers when he spoke. "I'm thinking about your skin."

"I like that," she said, because she really, truly did. It was sexy, erotic, and left all the right questions about what he was thinking sizzling in her mind.

He drew in a deep breath, stirring the hair near her temple. Her nipples hardened as if he'd used his tongue. And she swore her body was melting slowly from the inside out.

God, she was never going to last out the night.

Kelly John moved his mouth to hover at the edge of hers, took her wineglass from her hand, and whispered, "It's time."

She swallowed, nodded, swallowed again, and pushed

off the wall, reaching for his hand, which closed around hers as naturally as if she was right where she belonged.

Moisture seeped between her legs at the thought. Amazing, unexpected, and wonderfully, disarmingly real, her reaction to this man. Not that she was particularly surprised.

He'd caught her attention so long ago that this moment felt more like a prophecy fulfilled than an encounter happening only because of Kelly John's mistake.

She followed him around the wine bar, past the theater's concession stand, toward the rest rooms. He only glanced back once before pushing open a door she would've walked beyond without seeing. Considering it appeared to be part of the wall, she supposed she was forgiven.

The white lights overhead were glaringly bright, the floor industrial linoleum, the walls tinted just enough to be called off-white instead of snow. A set of swinging doors at the end obviously led into the kitchen.

Kelly John pulled her behind him into the short end of the corridor's "L", and backed her into the wall. His mouth came down on hers hard.

It was almost an assault. A desperate connection she wasn't sure she understood. She wondered if he did, but such wondering didn't stop her from kissing him back, from opening her mouth the way he seemed so insanely to need.

He pressed into her, his penis already thickly erect, already greedy, already seeking a fit. His tongue thrust into her mouth, his lower body thrust forward, and she spread her legs as far as her little black dress allowed.

Kelly John groaned and eased away, and she knew in that moment what had passed between them had nothing to do with the truth of why they were here.

A banquet chair cushioned in red velvet had been left toppled near the rear exit. Kelly John righted it, sat, turned her to scoot up and straddle his lap—a feat that wasn't accomplished without a major adjustment to her hemline.

By the time she settled onto his legs, her arms around his neck, her cleavage at mouth level, she could feel the cool air on her bottom as well as feel the heat from his thighs. She could also feel how very, very wet she was.

He slid his palms upward from her knees until he reached the tops of her stockings and her garters. He stared, his breathing rough and shallow, stared until she feared the vein at his temple would burst.

He closed his eyes then, dropped his head back until it hit the wall. "Emma?"

"Yes?" Her voice cracked on the one simple word.

"Is that all you're wearing under that dress?"

"The garter belt, you mean?"

He nodded, eyes still closed.

"No."

His lashes fluttered. His eyes slowly opened. He growled out, "What else?"

"A diamond stud in my navel."

He groaned, bit off a succinct, "Fuck me," that wasn't a request but a curse.

Her grin felt sly as it slid across her mouth. "I dressed with the cause in mind."

He opened one eye, lifted one brow. "The cause?"

"Anything to help."

"Christ, woman." Again with both closed eyes. "This kind of help and we might as well forget the whole thing."

"How so?"

"You're supposed to be saving me, not killing me."

She wanted to laugh but held back. "Oh, is that all?"

"All?" He lifted one of her hands away from his neck, lowered it to his lap, wrapped her fingers around his thick shaft and squeezed.

Only then did he open his eyes. "Like I said. You're killing me."

She couldn't help it. She squeezed again. He was long

and full and she wanted him. And so she let him go, took his hand in hers, and showed him quite clearly that he wasn't the only one hurting.

He hissed back a sharp breath, slicked a knuckle through the folds of her sex, brought the finger to his nose to smell, to his mouth to taste. Then he cupped the back of her head and kissed her.

She opened his jacket, curled her fingers into the silk of his shirt, went to work on the buttons because she was going to die if she didn't touch him.

One button, two buttons, three buttons, four was all it took before she could feel the soft dusting of hair over his pectoral muscles.

He'd crushed his mouth to hers, but she wasn't having any of it and tore away, kissing and biting her way down his throat, tonguing the dip beneath his Adam's apple, breathing him in.

He let her have her way for a few seconds more, and that was it. Holding her shoulders, he forced her up, sliding the fabric of her dress down her arms far enough to bind her—and to expose even more of her cleavage.

His eyes flashed as he held her gaze, as he slipped both hands beneath the scooped neckline and lifted her free. She watched his jaw tic, his temple throb.

And then he finally looked down.

He said things so raw, so coarse, yet so incredibly sexy that she blushed. The heat rose like a fever; she felt it on her skin and deep between her legs in a copious release of moisture.

Thank God it was dark outside and his pants were so very black.

It was when he leaned forward and pulled her nipple into his mouth so sharply and sweetly that she knew she was lost. She cried out before she could call back the sound.

He quickly released her, covered her mouth with his, and

swallowed the rest of the desperate whimpers that refused to be quieted.

This time he kissed her softly, gently, his lips catching hers, his tongue and teeth uninvolved. It was a lover's kiss, not one for show, not one for an audience, not one for a camera.

Her stomach tumbled, and she eased away. "Kelly?"

"Emma?"

She lowered her voice to a whisper. "This is going to sound incredibly stupid, but are we in the right place?"

His smile encompassed the whole of his face. "Got carried away and forgot that part, did you?"

"As a matter of fact . . ." She left it at that, knowing full well he knew that she had—and all that implied.

He nodded. "Trust me. You're exactly where I need you to be."

"If you're sure," she said, wanting to read more into his statement than was probably wise.

"I'm sure," he said, his hands on her thighs as he slouched back on his spine. "You know, I don't think I've ever had a woman wet my pants before."

She groaned. "I'm sorry. I should've warned you. Or at least worn more than I did."

He bit off one curse that was worse than the one he voiced. "Jesus H. Christ, Emma. Are you fucking kidding me? You're hot and you're gorgeous—"

"And I'm a mess."

He slid his hands higher, reaching beneath her dress and spreading her juices like he would finger paints. "A mess that I can't wait to lick up."

She held her breath, her hands on his shoulders, her arms pressing her bare breasts together. He caught her clitoris and squeezed.

"I want to taste you here." He slid the pads of two fingers along the inside walls of her slit, circled her vaginal entrance, and pushed deep. "I want to eat you up and fuck you with my tongue."

She nodded, she shook her head, she closed her eyes as he pulled out, eased back, again and again and again, increasing the speed and depth of his thrusts until she felt nothing but his fingers, and the tight spiraling heat in her core.

"Stop, please," she begged, opening her eyes once he no longer teased her. She panted a bit, gritted her teeth, whispered, "Not yet. I'm not ready."

A dark brow went up. Blue eyes twinkled. Dimples to die for appeared. "I hate to disagree, but I have the wet spot proving otherwise."

Cocky bastard. Arrogant, cocky ass. Damn him for being right. She moved her hands away from his shoulders, braced them on his thighs, made sure both of her nipples were gumdrop hard, and leaned forward.

"It's hardly fair that I have all the fun," she said, pleased to see he wasn't the god she'd been thinking, but a typical man brought to a state of mindless drooling by a little bit of flesh. "Kelly?"

"Emma?" he replied like a drone, looking up.

She made sure she had his attention, then asked, "How real do you need your alibi to be?"

He held her gaze for an interminable minute, one during which a war raged in his eyes, one fought between the will of his body and that of his mind.

It was obvious who won, and who lost, when he said, "I don't have a condom."

She didn't believe him. He was trying to spare her from something. Involvement. Embarrassment. She didn't know. She didn't care.

She wanted him because she wanted him and that was all that mattered.

The tapes were being made to save his life. As promised, they would be grainy, snowy, a low quality capable of identifying no one but Kelly John thanks to Tripp Shaughnessey's editing skills. He'd promised as well to angle the camera remotely and conceal her face.

Not all of her would be so obscured, however, and Tripp would see while working his editing magic. A fact she'd known and accepted when agreeing to this Mata Hari role. Making a vague fuzzy sex tape was, after all, all the rage.

As much as she wanted to make love to Kelly, she could live with that. She could live with anything as long as he gave in and filled her.

"I have condoms. In my purse." She canted her head, indicating her beaded clutch on the floor. And then she arched a brow. "Unless you're too camera shy."

Seven

Camera shy? That's what she wanted to know? If he minded showing off his dick on a videotape?

He narrowed his gaze, studied her face, read what he could of—and into—her expression. No, that wasn't what she was asking at all. She was daring him to let her seduce him.

And not a one of the arguments he'd given himself had yet to convince him to tell her to pack up her playthings and go.

Without breaking the lock he had on her gaze, he reached down for her purse. When he handed it to her, she straightened, her amazing tits bouncing into place.

Goddamn, but he couldn't wait to get her into a bed where he could show his appreciation of her assets properly. The thought sent his balls on another colorful rampage.

He swore he was going to burst.

Still, exposing her this way was unnecessary. For all the thoughts of blue balls and dying, he could wait.

She, however, seemed to be of a full-throttle mind, and held up the packet she'd pulled from her purse. "Shall I?"

He bit down hard on the imagined feel of her fingers. "We don't have to do this, Emma."

"I know we don't have to." Her eyelids fluttered. "I want to. I want to more than you probably know."

Oh, he knew. He was wearing the evidence. He shifted beneath her, holding onto her ass, which was barely covered by the hem of her dress.

He wanted to ask why, but at this point he didn't care about any of her reasons. He was a guy with a hard-on for the woman in his lap, and he was going to say yes no matter. But not without doing his best to protect her.

He shrugged out of his jacket and draped it over her shoulders, cocooning their bodies in the darkness inside. Only then did he reach for his belt buckle and zipper. Only then did he lift his hips, lower his pants, and let her set him free.

Her eyes widened, and he took the condom from her fingers and rolled it on. She scooted forward, raised her hips and her dress, settling the fabric around her waist and giving him the most glorious view of her garter belt and the sweet pink flesh of her sex.

"You're killing me here, Emma. You are fucking killing me."

She laughed softly. "Has anyone ever told you that your mouth would put a sailor's to shame?"

"You should hear what I don't say," he said as she reached between her thighs and spread herself open, showing him exactly where she wanted him to bury his thick, aching dick.

When he stared too long because he couldn't get enough of looking, she took him in her hand and guided him into place. He held onto the edges of his suit coat so that nothing got in the way of watching as she stretched open to take him inside.

He slid deep and settled, throbbing inside her, jaw tight, head pounding, fists crushing the fabric of his jacket into wadded, wrinkled balls.

But he kept his eyes wide open, and he drank his visual fill of this gift that only he could see. The tape would show nothing more explicit than Emma's bare breasts—an R-rated movie at best, fuzzy and indistinct.

And that was the last cognizant thought to cross his mind, because that was when Emma planted her hands on his knees, leaned back, and began to ride him like a trick pony.

She lifted her hips, lowered them, slid up and down the length of his shaft until the head of his cock was all of him she held inside.

He watched it all. Every slick stroke. Every centimeter she stretched to take him in. Every bit of it. He couldn't tear his eyes away from the picture of her gorgeous sex swallowing him from balls to tip.

Yet nothing could have prepared him for the look on her face when he finally tore his gaze from their joined bodies. Her eyes were glassy, her lips parted, the tip of her tongue pressed to the edge of her teeth.

She'd given herself to him completely, was taking from him all that she could. He thrust upward; she caught her weight in one hand, used the other to play her clit as she came.

She pressed her lips together, squeezed her eyes shut. Her contractions gripped him, his gut clenched, his abs contracted there in his open fly. He felt the vibrations of her silenced groans along the length of his cock.

She was finished, and now it was his turn. He released one corner of his jacket, cupped her head beneath her ponytail, and pulled her into his kiss. He needed her mouth to swallow the sounds bellowing up from his throat.

Needed her mouth as much as he needed her tight muscles milking his cock.

God-blessed-damn. He shot it all, thrusting once, twice, Emma squeezing and stroking, her free hand now playing nasty between their legs.

She fondled and fingered, and he opened up to her in ways that he'd never done with another woman. In ways, until now, he'd never thought he might like. He liked. A lot. She was fearless in her exploration.

And it was a long, long, long time before he let her out of his lap.

Hank Smithson had tired of pacing his office hours ago. Hell, he'd tired of pacing his office years ago, dad-blamed truth be told.

In fact, he'd pretty much tired of everything, doing no more these days than sitting back and letting his boys have all the fun.

Without his Madelyn around giving him a reason to keep his hands out of SG-5's fires, he saw no reason for things not to change.

And there was no better time than now. He glanced at his watch. Ten-thirty P.M. Kelly and Emma would be on their way to dinner.

And that meant Tripp Shaughnessey would be editing the images from the theater and the bar, images he'd captured with a few strategically located antennas borrowing bounced wireless feeds.

Hank didn't necessarily understand the workings of all the equipment his boys used. But he did understand that each and every one of them knew what they were doing.

And that was enough for him.

He stepped from the perimeter carpet that served as a sound buffer onto the tiles comprising the biggest part of the floor and made his way through the blacked-out ops center to the one desk in the horseshoe-shaped workstation still lit up like Times Square. Once there, he cleared his throat.

Tripp switched off the screen he'd been hunched over and swiveled his chair around. "Hank, hey. What's up?"

Hank nodded toward the dark monitor. "Things looking okay with Emma and Kelly?"

Tripp blinked, blushed, stammered, and stared before

snapping out of it. "Uh, yeah. It's going fairly damn well for K.J., I'd say."

"Good, good." Hank rolled the butt of his cigar from one corner of his mouth to the other. "He's getting what he needs then? To make this thing go away?"

"Oh, yeah," Tripp said. "End of the night? I think he'll have gotten exactly what he needs."

At the sound of the safety door opening, Hank and the now distracted Tripp both turned to see Julian Samms walk in.

"How're things going for K.J.?" he asked on his way to his desk.

"Right as rain," Tripp answered once Julian had adjusted his sling and situated himself in his chair. "What are you doing back here?"

"Katrina kicked me out." He flipped the switch for his main monitor, left the others dark. "She's on deadline and told me either I got my ass out or she was on the first flight back to Miami."

"Women," Tripp said. "Can't live with 'em, can't use 'em for a down payment on a new car."

"Depends on the dealership," Julian said and chuckled.

Hank did, too. He'd been having a hell of a good time lately watching his boys fall under the spells of a few good women. The team was mellowing out, settling down.

It was the perfect opportunity for him to get back to doing the things he'd been doing before a one of the boys had been born.

Emma savored the weight of Kelly John's palm in the small of her back as they followed the hostess to their table.

The light in the restaurant cast a pale amber glow over the room, each individual table illuminated by a small brass lantern centered in a fall-colored dried floral arrangement.

The intimate gentlemen's club ambience suited Emma's mood. She was strangely exhausted, and at the same time mellow. An obvious sex hangover. One curable only by sleep or by food.

She slipped into the booth the hostess indicated. The seat was a hunter green leather, and she sank deep and sighed.

Keeping her wits would've been so much easier sitting in one of the high-back club chairs at a table in the center of the room. Here she was, instead, fighting the temptation of sleep.

Kelly John slid his big body into the opposite seat, and the cozy space closed like a wool blanket around her. She loved the way it took him a minute to settle, adjusting the tails of his coat at his hips, his forearms on the table's edge as he discussed a pricey bottle with the wine steward.

Yet another glimpse into who he was. One that fit with the culturally urbane image of James Bond, yet seemed strangely anomalous when considering he could discuss Burgundies and Bordeaux with the same mouth capable of cursing a sailor under the table.

He caught her grinning like a schoolgirl with a crush when he glanced her way once the steward had gone.

"What?" he asked, the edge of his mouth tilted upward.

"What, what?" she asked in kind, tempted not just to sleep but to kiss him.

"You're staring."

She shrugged, teased. "I like looking at you. Have me arrested if it's that big of a problem."

This time he was the one staring, the one seemingly struck dumb by the concept that he made for tasty eye candy. Hard to believe of a man with this one's appeal to women.

She'd be surprised if he didn't have a woman in every port. And then it hit her, and she had to admit a bit of dislike for the idea of having become one of many.

Equally disconcerting was how her long dormant attraction, having surfaced, now felt like so much more than a simple appreciation of blue eyes and a very fine ass.

But the most disquieting of all was the way her heart refused to leave her throat for fear that the evening's inevitable end would be just that.

An end.

She couldn't accept that when their time tonight had stirred her blood so fiercely.

Finally, Kelly John shook his head. "Sorry. I'm still recovering from being totally blown away by the, uh, show at the theater."

She set her elbows on the table, laced her hands, rested her chin in the webbing of her fingers, and considered him. "I'm not sure if I should take that as a complaint or a compliment."

"A compliment definitely. It's just—"

He stopped as the wine steward arrived, presented the bottle, uncorked it, and poured with a subdued flourish suited to the flavor of the room.

Once he'd left them alone again, Kelly John studied the liquid in his glass as if waiting for it to turn into sacrificial blood. Her heart sank at his expression.

"Listen, Emma," he began, and she sat back and groaned. "Don't get me wrong. What happened back there at the theater . . ."

His sentence trailed, and she waited. She was not going to put words into his mouth or facilitate this confession that she didn't want to hear.

He lifted his glass, met her eyes over the rim. His expression was wary when he simply said, "It wasn't what I expected."

"You didn't enjoy it?"

"That's not what I said. It's just not what I'm used to."

"Which part would you not be used to?" she raised a brow to ask.

He leaned forward, spoke quietly. "A woman wanting sex for herself, instead of getting naked because she wants to get to me."

Now that was a strange admission. "Get to you how?"

He looked down to where his thumb rubbed over the grain in the table. And then he laughed to himself. "Who knows what evil lurks in the minds of women?"

Okay, this was too cute. Big bad Kelly John Beach was shy or embarrassed or both. "Watch it, mister. I've got one of those evil minds over here, and I'm not afraid to use it."

He chuckled again, but she sensed a hollowness to the sound, as if his thoughts had taken a solemn turn.

His words confirmed her intuition. "No. I don't think you will."

"So, then, if you don't think I'll use my mind . . . are you calling me an airhead?"

He collapsed back in the booth. "Jesus. A guy can't win for losing."

She grinned, loving how easy he was to disarm. "It's all about the battle of the sexes, sweetie."

"Yeah, well, I like to keep the war games out of my personal life," he said, and drank deeply of his wine.

She did no more than sip at hers, thinking. "You said earlier that you don't have girlfriends."

He nodded. "That I have sex."

"Right. Is that why? Because it's easier to bed a woman than to have to talk to her?"

He leaned forward and signaled her close with a crook of his finger. For the first time since this charade began, she felt threatened. Not by his intimidating presence, but by the truth of who and what he was.

By the beast inside him that was able to live on the periphery of involvement in order to do what he needed to do. The one she'd welcomed into her body, and now found herself embracing with her heart.

So when he spoke, she did more than hear his words. She listened.

"Talking to a woman means getting to know her, enjoying her as a friend, as a lover, falling in love, then coming home to her in however many body bags it takes to hold all the parts. And I'm not going to do that to any woman. Ever."

That said, he cupped the back of her head and he kissed her.

Eight

Women. Had to get all hepped up about relationships and ruin a good physical thing.

He'd been officially introduced to Emma less than six hours ago, and she was already judging him because he preferred his sex without strings.

No matter how many times or in how many ways he explained why things had to be the way they were, she would never understand. Not when she couldn't know what it took to do the things he did. The things he had to do.

Things that ripped him up so goddamn badly at times that he would rather die than ever share the brutality with a woman he loved. No woman deserved having his fucked-up shit dumped in her lap.

He shared it with Tripp, and with the other Smithson Group members to a lesser extent. But the truth went no further. Neither did his trust. It couldn't.

He'd learned his lesson in Nicaragua and wasn't about to put himself in such a bad place again.

He climbed behind Emma into the backseat of the taxi that rolled up then, and slammed the door. The driver pulled away from the restaurant. At Kelly John's side, Emma sat silent, much as she had during their meal.

He'd never have thought he could shut her up with a kiss, but once she'd managed to stop tickling the back of his throat with her tongue, they'd talked of next to nothing.

All they'd done was order and discuss insignificant crap, though the conversation had gotten a bit more personal, had felt a bit more comfortable, more natural, than any of the others they'd shared.

After what had gone down between them in the theater, that hardly came as a surprise—though he had to admit the aftermath had caught him off guard. Sex with Emma hadn't been the sort that ended once he'd pulled up his pants.

And that was a new experience, the fact that he hadn't wanted to hit the door running before she could beg him to stay.

He slouched back, spread his legs, stared sightlessly out the window at his side, hoping Tripp's hack into the restaurant's camera system had captured the kiss at least. Otherwise . . . hell.

There was no otherwise. He'd completely blown it. No seizing the opportunity. No focusing on the endgame. Oh, no. None of that.

He'd been too weirded out by the tension to think straight, to step up the plan. His balls were in a vise, and he'd just ratcheted the damn thing up tight.

He'd seen Emma before, of course. He didn't walk into Hank's office wearing blinders when he had business there. He'd seen her, and he knew she'd seen him.

But it was that shared sort of seeing that had nothing to do with looking at each other and everything to do with the air in the room being impossible to breathe.

Hank's suggestion to bring her in on this scheme had caused a hitch in his side for more reasons than not wanting to put her in danger.

Spending up-close-and-personal time with the only woman in a long time to snag his interest outside of his pants scared the holy hell out of him.

When he felt her shift at his side, felt her sidle up closer and slip her arm around his neck, his antennae popped. He glanced over, found her lips inches away, leaned his head down so she could whisper into his ear.

"Don't look now but I think we have a rapt audience."

"How's that?" he whispered back.

"I've caught the driver using his rearview mirror a lot more than seems necessary."

He straightened, catching the driver's dark-eyed gaze from beneath his turban almost immediately, waiting another two, three, four heartbeats before turning his attention back to Emma.

He crooked his finger, teased her over, stroked the column of her neck from her chin to the hollow of her throat, and brushed his lips to her ear. "Taking this spy business to heart, are you?"

"Just call me Mata Hari," she said, turning so that her lips hovered near his.

He pulled her closer, cutting his gaze back to the mirror where again the driver's interest seemed way more than casual. Seemed too sharp, too interested.

The possibility that the man was Spectra flashed briefly through Kelly John's mind. They'd had the same eighteen hours to get to him that he'd had to throw them off track.

The plan was that he and Emma were dating, that their sex tapes were recorded last night. A second night spent doing the hot-and-heavy made perfect sense as a continuing cover.

Or so he tried to rationalize as a way of getting his hands on her again. "Hmm. Mata Hari used seduction as a tool of the trade, right?"

Emma nodded. The tip of her tongue darted out to tickle the edge of his mouth. "If you want me, all you have to do is tell me."

"God, Emma." Wanting her the way he did should've made it easier to gear up for another show. But it didn't.

Because what he wanted was to have her all to himself. No cameras, no observers, no scenario to play out.

Nothing but the two of them alone in her bed.

He nuzzled her neck, breathed her in, thought about retiring and living to a ripe old age and never again dealing with misplaced trust. "I want you, Emma."

"I want you, too."

"But what we do here is for him. Not for me. Later it will be for me."

She sighed with a breathy shiver. "Oh, Kelly, it's about damn time."

He chuckled, drawing her body across his lap. Her backside settled between his spread legs. "What's that supposed to mean, about damn time?"

She wiggled close to him, laced her hands behind his neck. "I've had the hots for you for years."

His cock began to swell. But the swelling he really felt was happening higher. Right in the center of his chest. "The hots, huh?"

She nodded, reached up and sprinkled kisses over his neck. "This was all before I knew that you shared Pat Benatar's take on things."

"Come again?" he asked, on his way to another superb hard-on.

She dipped her tongue beneath his shirt collar. "Thinking that love is a battlefield."

Love. That helped put a damper on things. "Isn't it?"

"I like to think of it more as a contact sport. Besides, this is more about lust than anything, isn't it?"

"It's more about something," he said because he was pretty sure it wasn't only about two hot and horny bodies.

She pulled back to look at him. "Oh, that's very definitive."

"What do you want me to say? We just met."

"Right. And this is just about me helping to save your ass."

It had started out that way. Or so he wanted to convince himself. Now it was all about how he seemed to have met his match. How much he was suddenly thinking out of his short-term box. How much he wanted to kiss her.

And so he did.

His hand on the back of her head, he lifted her to meet his descending mouth. And then he kissed her like all that mattered was losing himself in what she made him feel. In the way she made him forget.

He knew nothing but her touch, the stroke of her tongue, her taste. He felt as much as heard her desperate whimpers, swearing he could smell her arousal when that much was no doubt imagined.

Imagined and anticipated because he knew her amazing way of letting go, the mind-blowing response of her body.

She was unlike any woman he'd known at any time in his past, and that got to him in ways he should've been beyond being able to feel.

It was a feeling he wanted to explore. A feeling he wanted to trust when his idea of trust had long ago ceased to exist.

What he felt now was her hand inside his jacket, her fingers smoothly releasing the buttons of his shirt, threading into his chest hair, working down toward his belt buckle. He stopped her before she got that far. The theater had been iffy; this definitely was not the time or the place.

Besides, right now? All he wanted was her kiss. Or so he told himself until she stroked her tongue over his in a motion that had him thinking how it would feel with her lips loving him elsewhere.

He groaned, and she chuckled, easing back to kiss the barest edge of his mouth. "You amaze me. Every time you kiss me, it's like the first time."

"Yeah, well, I aim to please." Lame, but he couldn't think of anything else to say.

She smoothed down and patted his jacket's lapels. "Your aim is perfect. It's your attitude needing an adjustment."

"That so?"

She nodded and this time caressed his jaw. "I'll see what I can do about that."

He snorted, but only meant half of it. God, she couldn't keep her hands off him; how could he possibly be of a mind to argue? "Think you're the woman for the job?"

She captured his gaze, arched one brow. The light was dim, but enough for him to see the twinkle beneath. "I knew that even before you hired me."

The car began to slow. He had no time to respond to her comment—a very good thing because he was clueless on how to react. The same cocky attitude in another woman would've had him on a fast boat to as far away as he could get.

But Emma wasn't any other woman. For now, she was his.

She scooted out of his lap, straightened her hair and her hemline while the driver eased the car to the curb in front of her place.

Kelly John sat forward on full alert. If the driver was working for Spectra and was doing more than observing, now would be when he'd make his move. But he did nothing more than wait for his fare, allowing Kelly John to breathe easier.

None of their conversation had been loud enough to be overheard, though being picked up by a parabolic mike wasn't out of the question.

Emma had followed his lead and said nothing beyond what a lover might say. She'd played her part perfectly, given him the alibi he needed.

What happened now, once upstairs in her apartment, was off the books.

It wasn't until after he'd paid the fare and the taxi pulled away that he snapped to the fact that more than a few things were off.

The driver had no beard, but wore a Sikh's turban with

what looked like dreadlocks snaking out from beneath. But it was the single diamond stud in his earlobe that gave Kelly John pause.

Dreadlocks and diamonds . . .

Jesus H. Christ. Standing in the middle of the street, his heart thundering, he pulled out his satellite phone and dialed, making a connection the NSA would kill to listen in on—if they could track it down.

In the ops center, Julian Samms answered. Kelly John gave him time to do no more than identify himself before saying, "Your Spectra assassin. From Miami? He's here."

"*Ta ma de wang ba dan.* What? Where?"

"On Bank Street. In the West Village. Behind the wheel of a taxi."

Nine

Emma tossed her bag on the entry table in what served as her apartment's foyer, kicked off her shoes as she walked through the living room, and welcomed the cool tile on her stockinged feet once she reached the kitchen.

She heard the catch of the front door echo behind her and braced herself for the inevitable. She had no idea what had happened out there in the street, but this evening would be coming to a quick end if Mr. Strong-and-Silent didn't get with the program.

Whether he liked it or not, she'd left her need-to-know basis behind the moment she'd sat in his lap and opened herself to him body and soul. What she feared was that he was stuck on the body part and hadn't snapped to the fact that making love wasn't a case of taking one for the team.

She'd made love with him because she'd known from the moment of walking into Hank's office and finding Kelly John there she would not be waking up in the morning to the same life she'd lived for the past five years.

It was time to find out exactly what she'd gotten herself into. And where she was headed after tonight, since there was no going back.

She poured filtered water and measured chocolate truffle

decaf into the coffeemaker's basket, listening for Kelly John, assuming he'd join her once he took care of business.

A business that had seemed a novelty when she'd signed up for a crash course earlier tonight. A business she now realized wasn't a business at all.

It was his life.

It wasn't play-acting, or an on-again, off-again adventure to seize. Kelly John's blood pulsed red with danger. He breathed it in the way she breathed in air.

The realization humbled her. That he took on so much, sacrificed so much, with no compensation or praise? Her throat ached at the thought.

The coffeemaker started in with its hissing and steaming and gurgling. She breathed in the brew's sweetly earthy aroma and swore again that, decaf or not, coffee was the nectar of the gods.

With a cup in hand, she could face anything. Even the man behind her now, filling the room with his bulk and an equally large wave of tension sending nerves to flutter between her legs in tender anticipation.

"Smells good," he said, sounding as sincere as most efforts at making pleasantries.

"It'll probably smell better once you splash it with Kahlua." She turned and leaned back against the countertop, her hands at her sides and curled over the edge. "Unless you prefer not to drink on the job?"

He grunted, crossed his arms, faced her. "I'm pretty sure I didn't kill that bottle of wine at dinner alone."

"True. But with whatever it is that's come up now"—and she hated how he'd pushed her into the building while he handled his issue with the driver of the cab—"I thought you might need more of your wits about you."

"Whatever it is that's come up now has been taken care of."

No. She wasn't going to let him off that easy. He wanted

to share her bed, he needed to know more about who she was. To realize she wouldn't be satisfied with pat answers.

"Tell me something, Kelly."

"Shoot."

"The work you do. Is it really ever taken care of?"

He paused, responded, "Are you pissed about something, Emma? Because I sure as hell can show myself to the door."

Avoidance had to be the man's fourth name. "Is that what you want? To go?"

"No. It's not what I want."

She offered him a small smile. "Good. I don't want that either."

"But you do want something." His blue eyes flashed with a brutal challenge. "Besides coffee and Kahlua."

She considered him, nodded. "I want to know you. In more than the biblical sense."

"There's not a lot to know."

"Spoken like a man."

"Argued with like a woman."

"And so the war games begin."

He dropped his head back, closed his eyes, breathed deep. "This was a mistake."

"What? Coming here? Or thinking that shortcutting the steps to intimacy meant we wouldn't have to back up and deal with the parts that aren't quite so much fun?"

"That's not it," he said, looking at her once again.

"Then the mistake was me thinking that after what we've shared tonight, you might want to know me better." She shrugged. "Wishful thinking and all that, I suppose."

"No, Emma. It's not wishful thinking. I do want to know you."

"It can only work both ways, Kelly." She hesitated, wanting to say the right thing, wanting to assure him of . . . something. Her allegiance. Her sincerity. She wasn't even sure what emotion it was binding her chest so tightly.

"I trusted you tonight not to let me get hurt. Can't you trust me not to hurt you?"

He shook his head as he answered. "I'm not sure I can trust anyone that far. Not anymore."

"Not even the other guys on your team?"

"I trust them."

"Then trust me. Think of me as a junior member."

He chuckled lightly at that. "That's not as simple as it sounds. I share a locker room with them. And I'd rather not picture you with a hairy ass."

He was so cute when he grinned that she had a really hard time not jumping into his arms. She wanted to share more with him than physical bliss. And to get there, they had to talk.

She turned to take down two mugs from the cabinet above the coffeemaker. Kelly John moved in behind her, bracing his hands on the countertop, effectively imprisoning her with his size and a strength that might have intimidated her had she not figured out how gentle he was hours ago.

She started to object, to put him into his place, but he nuzzled the skin beneath her ear so sweetly that all she could do was sigh.

"You gotta know, Emma. Trust doesn't come easy for me anymore." He laughed deep in his chest; the rumble tickled her back. "I'm pretty blown away by the fact that you managed to get to me as completely as you did."

"It's good to know you're capable of letting your guard down," she said, and shivered because of what he was doing to her ear.

"Surprised the hell out of me." He nuzzled lower, working his way down her neck and toward her shoulder where the neckline of her dress barely hung on.

No. *No, no, no.* She was not going to let him distract her to the point of losing sight of what she wanted.

"But it surprised me even more how much I found myself wanting to tell you everything. About the team I led in Nicaragua, and the end of my military career."

"You can tell me now." She held one of the mugs so tightly she wondered if it would crack before she could pour. "I'll pour your coffee—"

"I don't want any coffee. I only want you."

His words hung in the room with a bitter desperation; she set the cup on the countertop and turned in his arms. Before she could say anything, his hands were at the hem of her dress, pulling it up her thighs, over her hips, bunching the fabric at her waist and baring her below.

She couldn't think to stop him as he dropped to his knees. She could only close her eyes, spread her legs, and grip the edge of the countertop as if nothing else would keep her from falling.

He parted the lips of her sex with his thumbs, ran the flat of his tongue through her folds. He circled her clit, sucked the hard knot into his mouth, released her before she could cry out, and moved deeper between her legs.

It was a wild and crazy ride and she wanted him with her. Wanted him inside of her. Wanted him to know the same beauty, the rightness of what she felt with his tongue pushing deep.

She grabbed the shoulders of his jacket and urged him up. He was frowning when he stood, yet she couldn't afford the time it would take to explain.

All she knew was that she needed him out of his clothes, his pants around his knees, his thick cock sliding into her, soothing the nerve endings that had her on fire.

She reached for his belt buckle. He beat her to it, chuckling as she whispered, "Hurry, hurry," and shucking down his pants. His erection thrust forward beneath the lowest button on his shirt, and she thought she would die.

He was thick, ripe like a plum and almost as purple. She wanted him in her mouth, but later, later. Right now her need was as elemental as need could possibly be.

She hooked a leg around his hips; he cupped her bottom,

lifted her, spread her open, stopped only to growl out, "Are you sure?"

She'd never been more sure of anything, and she begged, "Yes, oh, yes. Fuck me, please."

He plunged deep and hit bottom. She cried out, leaned back, braced her upper body weight on her elbows while he held her lower half, his fingers digging into the backs of her thighs as he filled her with a fierceness that frightened her, that thrilled her.

Because it was the fierceness of a man's emotion, and she knew she was falling in love.

"Your body is fabulous, did you know that?"

Emma didn't care what Kelly John thought or even whether or not he answered since she was talking mostly to herself. She couldn't get enough of touching him.

His skin, and all the textures of his hair—on his chest like fine silk, in the pits of his arms, coarse like straw, and cushioning his penis, thick and wiry.

He was a mosaic of hard and soft, of unexpected dips and crevices, bumps and scars, a patched-up, stitched-up, Humpty Dumpty map of the life he'd lived. He made her feel like the time she'd served behind bars had been spent in a spa.

"Well, your body is pretty fucking hot itself," he finally answered from where he lay beneath her.

She sat straddling his thighs, and was doing her best to learn all she could of how he felt, using her fingers and thumbs, the heels of her palms, her knuckles.

At his typically Kelly John comment, she gave up her exploration of his amazing abs and the silky dark hair that covered them, crossed her arms beneath her bare breasts, and sat back.

"You'll catch more flies with honey than with that filthy mouth of yours."

"And who was it begging for it in the kitchen a while

ago?" He reached up and pulled her hands away from her breasts. "Seems your mouth isn't much cleaner than mine, sweetheart."

God, what they'd done in the kitchen. So hard and wild and out-of-her-league explosive she'd barely been able to walk to the bedroom once they were done.

Thinking of it even now, she felt the rising heat of a blush, certain it was staining her face, glad the only light shining over the bed came from the bathroom door left ajar.

His directness, his bluntness excited her, left her nearly unable to breathe.

He was so unlike the men she knew and dated, so intense, larger than life . . .

It was just as she'd determined earlier. From here on, nothing in her life would ever be the same—even knowing how far they had to go.

And because of that . . .

She laced her fingers with his, pinned his hands on the mattress at his shoulders, leaned forward, glared down. "You think that was dirty? You haven't heard nothin' yet."

He laughed. The sound rumbled through her limbs, into her belly where it took hold and blossomed. "You sure talk tough for a naked woman."

"You want tough?" She gripped his hands harder, squeezed his fingers tighter, pushed him down into the mattress with all the strength produced by her months of weight lifting. "I'll give you tough."

"Bring it on, woman."

"Fine. But don't say I didn't warn you."

He bucked his naked lower half up against her. His penis slapped against her belly. "I'm shaking in my combat boots."

"As well you should be, considering I'm about to take you down," she said, though from her vantage point it didn't seem his boots were what was shaking.

"Yeah, you and whose army?"

She sat back, narrowed her eyes, and glared down. If it

was a battle he wanted . . . "It won't take an army to ask you what I want to know."

He stilled. He response was slow in coming, and then was a deep, "Uh-oh."

She crossed her arms over her chest. "Waving a white flag already?"

He didn't respond, but she heard the pop of his jaw as he ground his teeth and braced for the blow.

"I want to know what the hell happened to make you give up on the idea of love."

Ten

He lay there unmoving, wondering when his heart would start beating again, when his lungs would voluntarily expand.

When his muscles would relax so he could move off the bed and out the door, grab his clothes from wherever he'd left them, and find a sewer where he wouldn't have to worry about spilling his guts.

"Did I ever say I believed in love in the first place?" he finally asked, losing the really nice erection he'd had going on at the mental image of the rats and the stench below the street. At the thought of leaving here for there.

Of leaving here at all.

"Oh, Kelly. You're too passionate for me to believe otherwise." She rushed on before he could stop her. "And don't feed me that line about having sex and not relationships."

"It's not a line."

"It is when you use it on me as an excuse to get out of telling me the truth."

He shifted up onto his elbows, not liking the idea of bolting, but knowing if she didn't drop it . . . "I did tell you the truth."

"Right. That thing about the body bags."

"That's not truth enough for you?"

"No, Kelly. That's your truth. It's the reason you give yourself for not getting involved."

"It's a pretty damn good one if you ask me."

"Why don't you let me decide that? Why not give me a chance to use my head and decide what I'm willing to risk?"

Why was she yammering on? Why couldn't she let it go? He didn't think he'd ever known a woman so bent on having her way. "You wouldn't know what you're risking. You don't know what I do."

"Do cops' wives know? Firefighters' wives?" She paused, let that settle. "I can't know if you don't tell me. And if you don't tell me something, anything, give me a hint at least of where you're coming from, how will I ever know who you are?"

He snorted. "You want that? To know who I am? What I've done?"

"I want to know you," she said, her voice soft, gentle, her fingertips swirling lightly through the hair covering his abs. "I want to know you."

Would talking help? Would it hurt? Would it make any difference? He'd never thought so before. He didn't think so now.

But he didn't want her to force him to find his clothes. He didn't want her to send him on his way. He didn't want to leave—not because of the rats and the sewer, but because this and no place else was where he wanted to be.

Fuck it, but he did not want to have to do this. He did not. He did not. *He did not.*

But he knew then that he was going to.

"I can't tell you a lot of it." The missions he'd run were called black ops for a reason. "It's not you, and it's not any Skull and Bones brotherhood. It's just that a lot of what I've done doesn't exist."

"Black ops."

He rolled his eyes at Miss Know-It-All. "I don't talk about those days before Hank found me. I won't. I can't. Except to say that I saw too much. I did too much."

He bit down on his tongue but was way too late in doing so. "I killed a man in cold blood."

She remained unmoving for a moment that seemed to last forever. And when he was opening his mouth to answer the rats who were calling his name, she slid from his lap to the bed.

She stretched out alongside him, her toes tickling his calf, her hands clasped between her breasts, her breath warm on his shoulder.

"What happened?"

"It wasn't enemy fire. It wasn't friendly fire. It was me thinking about it long and hard beforehand." He squeezed his eyes shut, opened them just as quickly.

He would much rather look at her ceiling than at the memories etched into his eyelids. Memories of the whites of Randy Shield's eyes as the garrote bit through his neck.

Kelly John swallowed hard, cleared his throat. "It was me knowing that it was either take him down or lose my entire squad."

"Because of what he did."

A nod, though he doubted she could see. "He'd broken rank, betrayed our trust. It was kill or be killed."

"Then you did what you had to do."

"Or so I've spent a hell of a lot of years trying to convince myself." And, all the while, hating himself for taking a man's life. Hating the other man for the greed and the weakness that left so many lives ruined.

His might not be at the top of the list, but it sure as hell felt that way deep in his gut. "It would've been better if I'd never trusted him in the first place. He was new in country. New to the outfit. I should've known better."

God, to put even that much into words, to look back and relive, to wonder and doubt and hate. He raised the arm nearest Emma, draped his wrist over his eyes.

He couldn't say anymore. Couldn't look at anymore of the past.

Beside him, Emma snuggled nearer, laid her head on his biceps, her palm in the center of his chest. She didn't say anything. She didn't rub or stroke or caress.

She simply held the echo of his heartbeat close and warmed him with her soul.

It was almost dawn when Kelly John woke, surprised he'd slept at all. Even more surprised to find himself spooned up against a very naked Emma beneath her quilt.

The four hours of shut-eye he'd had felt like eight. He'd slept so deeply, rested so completely that he doubted he'd even dreamed.

Now, of course, he was hard beyond belief with the need to pee. He eased away from her softness and warmth, and immediately felt the loss.

A loss that startled him since he was used to sleeping alone.

He flipped off the bathroom light before pushing open the door. He wanted Emma to sleep until he could get back and wake her up right.

The frosted glass window was gray with the beginning of the day, and he saw well enough to do his business. He even remembered to put the seat down once he was done.

The thought almost made him laugh. And since when did he laugh when standing naked in a bathroom, his dick in his hand? All he knew was that last night, the moment he'd stepped through Emma's door, his world had somehow righted.

He padded his way across her bedroom's hardwood floor, crawled under the quilt on his hands and knees, and waited until she stirred and rolled onto her back before scooting up to straddle her body.

"Morning, sleepyhead."

"It's not morning," she groused. "It's dark outside. Go away."

He chuckled to himself, leaned down and kissed the pooch of her belly just beneath her navel, doing it again when she groaned.

"Stop kissing my fat. Go away."

"Sounds like the efficient Emma Webster is not a morning person."

"What time is it?" she grumbled. He felt her squirrel around to look at the clock. This time when she groaned she shook the whole bed. "You'd better have a damn good reason for being down there. It's not even six o'clock."

He dipped his lower body, slid his cock up the length of her thigh. "Is that a good enough reason?"

She waited until her body had stopped trembling before she told him, "No. It's not."

It was, and she knew it. Hell, he knew she knew it because she hadn't been able to keep her voice from cracking. Still, he was game to play by her rules. He'd be claiming his prize his way in the end.

He scooted lower, kissed her lower, his balls tucked tightly against her leg, the soft hair not waxed away tickling his chin.

She pushed against his knees where his legs held hers together, where he'd restricted her movement in a teasing upper hand.

When she pushed a second time with more force and a fierce growl, he let her have her way, lifting one knee then the other and setting her free.

She spread her legs wide, pulled her heels toward her hips. Her knees tented the quilt and gave him room to do his work. Work that was so much more pleasure than effort.

She smelled incredible. Salty and sweet, like the sun-warmed sea. He nuzzled the lips of her sex and breathed her in, feeling his cock bob up into his belly, feeling the extension of his erection thicken all the way to his ass.

He circled her clit with his tongue, flicked it with butter-fly touches, sucked it into his mouth with just enough pressure to bring her hips off the bed—and then he let her go.

He'd make sure she came later. He had too much of her yet left to eat.

His weight braced on his elbows, he slid his thumbs through her folds, pulled back the hood protecting her clit. She was bare, fully exposed, laid open from her belly to her sweet, juicy entrance.

He waited, doing nothing but nuzzling her tender thighs, letting her arousal build and race like wildfire. He could taste it on the surface of her skin, that electric sizzle, that metallic tang.

He could smell it, the shift in her scent from budding to rich and ripe. And now he was the one who could no longer wait. He sucked at her flesh there, thick with the rush of blood through her veins, and thrust his tongue inside her.

She arched up, begging, writhing, her flesh sweet with her arousal's moisture. He returned his mouth to her clit, used her slick cream to wet his fingers, to slide one then a second into her body as far as he could.

He drew on the hard knot, sucked it between his lips, pushing his thumb inside of her, circling a finger over the bud of her ass. She exploded. He felt her spasms everywhere he touched her.

She shuddered, shook, clenched up tight, closing around his fingers, her contractions pushing, pulling, gripping, and calming at last.

An *at last* that he hated to see happen. He loved knowing how much pleasure she took in his touch. And even if her completion meant it was his turn to get started.

As if reading his mind, she stretched her legs, reached down between his and cupped his heavy sac. The only thing she said was, "Mmm," but he thought he might unload at the deep throaty sound.

He didn't move, just sat back on his heels and let her stroke him. The head of his cock felt like a ripe apple ready to burst from its skin. When she thumbed the slit in the tip and swirled the beaded moisture, he was done for.

He pried her hands from his body, moved them to her breasts, and crawled up to straddle her ribcage. He didn't say a word. He couldn't.

He'd wanted to be here like this from the first moment he'd seen her gorgeous tits straining to pop out of her dress.

The room had lightened enough that he could see in her eyes her awareness of what he wanted, and she tucked a pillow beneath her head and smiled.

He moved further up her body, curled his hands over the top railing of her wrought iron headboard, and started to thrust into the valley where she pressed her breasts together.

He took it slow to start with, his eyes rolling back at the feel of her plump tits held so tight and so close that he could hardly fit between.

But then she opened her mouth, flicked her tongue over the tight skin covering the head of his cock each time it came close, and slow turned into an effort in futility.

His hold on the headboard became a death grip as he pumped harder, faster. Her tits squeezed him, her lips sucked him. He trailed a sticky string of jiz over her skin as he listened to her beg him to fuck her.

The bed shook with the rhythm of his hips. He stared down, watching her tweak at her nipples, watching his cock slide between her breasts and into her mouth, watching the *come-to-mama* circle she formed with her lips and the licking crook of her tongue.

That was it. His fantasy of the perfect woman's wet, willing, and welcoming mouth. And the next thing he found himself watching was his come filling the bowl of her tongue before she sucked him to the back of her throat.

She swallowed him from head to balls, her cheeks milking him dry. He shuddered, felt the squeezing contractions deep between his legs until he was spent and drained with nothing more to give.

He waited a moment, finally moving when the sweat beaded on his forehead threatened to drip onto hers. Only then did he find the strength to slide beneath the covers and spoon against her.

He wanted to thank her, but didn't want her to think his appreciation was all about the sex. It was, but it was also so very much more, and at the top of the list was the lesson in trust.

She'd flipped the switch on a megawatt spotlight and forced him to face the monsters in his closet. The difference this time was that she'd stayed beside him from the moment he'd opened the door.

And now, for the first time since Nicaragua, he felt he might actually relax enough to catch up on years' worth of missed sleep.

Eleven

Emma left Kelly John sleeping while she showered in the guest bathroom. She ended up going through her morning routine in silence once she'd gathered her things, having closed the bedroom door for a second time without waking him.

She dressed in the guest room, pulled her hair back with a clip instead of dealing with hot rollers, did her makeup at the kitchen table while drinking her coffee, totally skipping Katie and Matt.

The fact that Kelly was sleeping as hard as he was meant a lot—primarily that he didn't do it often enough and that his body wasn't going to let him get by on catnaps one more day.

To Emma, that said that his mind had waited until feeling safe before shutting down. And she liked that. She liked it a lot. Liked that she'd created a place where he'd been able to let down his guard.

A place in her bed, in her heart. In her life.

She'd never bought into the silliness of love at first sight. The concept was out of step with her belief that a lasting relationship took time, required nurturing, began with shared interests and mutual respect—not with garter belts worn sans panties and boxer briefs shoved to the knees.

Even now, on her way out the door, the consummate executive assistant in navy Liz Claiborne and Prada pumps, she shivered before she managed to tamp down the memory. There was a time and place for fantasizing, but if she didn't get her act in gear she would miss the bus and be late.

With five minutes to spare, she exited the elevator onto the twenty-third floor of the financial district high-rise housing Smithson Engineering, and made her way to the executive suite.

Hank's door was standing open, and seeing her walk by, he waved her in. She tucked her purse and workout bag beneath her desk's kneehole and took a deep breath, feeling less like Mata Hari this morning than like the daughter who didn't have permission to bring her boyfriend home.

So much for Liz Claiborne and Prada and being all grown up.

"Good morning, sir," she said cheerily. "Are you needing Starbucks as much as I am?"

Hank came out from behind his desk chuckling. "You and your big budget coffee. I suppose you'll be needing a raise soon to support your habit."

She hesitated; before last night, his comment would not have tickled so much as a hair on one eyebrow. Now her entire nape was tingling.

Surely he wasn't offering to pay her for the services she'd rendered last night to Kelly?

Oh, God. Please don't let him have seen how far she'd taken her charge. She swallowed her unease, smiled. "Annual reviews began the first of next month. I think I can hold out until then."

"Good, good." He nodded, distracted. "Things went okay last evening? You had a good time?"

"I had a very good time, yes. Thanks so much for getting

us the table at the restaurant." Keep it light, keep it friendly. That she thought she could do.

"I knew getting reservations so late wasn't going to happen without a bit of string pullin'," he said, perching his good hip on the edge of his desk and crossing his arms.

She offered a nodding bow. "The strings were much appreciated. And the beef was to die for."

"Pricey stuff, that Kobe. But worth every penny."

She laughed. "As long as the pennies are coming out of your pocket, I'd have to agree."

"Speakin' of out of pocket." He cleared his throat nervously. "You haven't by any chance seen Kelly since last night, have you?"

She curled her fingers over the back of the visitor's chair behind which she stood, stared down at the seat. "Yes, as a matter of fact. It was late when we got in, and he stayed at my place. He was still sleeping, actually, when I left this morning."

When she looked up again, she found Hank's complexion colored a ruddy red. He covered the moment with a cough made behind his fist. "Well, it's good the boy's getting some rest. I worry that he doesn't do that enough."

"Did you need him? I can call the house and see if he's awake," she said, realizing how lame the offer was when Hank would no doubt have all manner of ways to make contact.

He lifted his hip from his desk, waved off her suggestion. "I'll catch up with him later."

She nodded. "Do you need anything done this morning before I get back to yesterday's EPA reports?"

"Yes." He narrowed one eye and pointed. "I need you to get your coffee before Starbucks closes up shop for lack of business."

She laughed. And she did.

*   *   *

The morning passed quickly after that. Emma barely looked up before lunch. She wanted to say that she hadn't stopped at all to wonder where Kelly John was and what he was doing, but she'd never understood the benefit of lying to oneself.

She'd thought of him constantly, wondered if this current job, the one putting his butt in a sling, required he come into the office.

Or if he'd be in only if he needed to get with Tripp on the tapes, with Hank on where the assignment went from here. With the group if they held regular briefings in that amazing room on the twenty-fourth floor.

Strange, perhaps, but working with him on a need-to-know basis had allowed her to quash her curiosity about what it was he'd been caught doing.

It was only now, with all said and done, that she had the presence of mind to consider what it was she'd helped save him from.

Honestly, though, she wasn't sure it made a difference. She wasn't even sure she really cared.

All that mattered was that last night produced the hoped-for results, and that Kelly John was now out of harm's way—a twofold wish of sorts, because she wanted him safe for her as much as for himself.

He was the man she'd been looking for all of her life, the man she wanted in her life. She didn't need to slow down and first nurture what they had.

The twelve hours they'd spent together felt richer and more emotionally complete than she would have believed possible yesterday in Hank's office when they'd been introduced.

Knowing the truth now made her anxious to get back to him, to see him again, to make him pecan waffles and serve him in bed.

In fact . . . She glanced at her watch as the second hand swept from the five to the ten. Yes! Why not? It was close enough to lunchtime. She wouldn't be able to stay home long, of course . . . She supposed she should call, though surprising him would be much more fun.

And, if he wasn't there, she'd gather up the dry cleaning needing to be done. A perfect plan—especially going in as she was with no expectations.

If he was gone? She'd simply see him later. She reached for her purse first, then the phone.

"Hank, here."

"Sir, I'm going to take an early lunch. Would you like anything before I go?"

"I'm fine, Emma. Not much of an appetite quite yet. Maybe I'll walk down to Brighton's when you get back."

"All right. I'll be back as soon as I can," she said, hoping that the busses were running on schedule, that she had everything to make waffles, that Kelly John was still there.

Once out of the executive wing and into the lobby, she found only one elevator moving between floors. Since she was leaving for lunch early, the wait wasn't long, though she hated losing even two minutes.

The car finally arrived, and she stepped inside to ride down with one other passenger. He slouched back in one corner, ankles crossed, hands braced on the car's railing holding his weight.

From the one brief glance she'd taken, he appeared to be watching the panel's digital display.

It was hard to tell with the dark glasses he wore.

They began the descent, Emma holding the narrow strap of her purse hooked over her shoulder, finding herself impatiently flexing her fingers around the leather and staring at the floor numbers as well.

Staring until she sensed movement from her co-rider, who pushed off the back wall on which he was leaning and pressed the emergency stop button.

What the hell? She raised her gaze from his hand on the button to his face. Took a step away as he pulled the reflective lenses from his face.

"Excuse me?" she began, stopped by the shake of his head and the silencing finger he pressed to his lips.

Or so she thought, until she realized what had silenced her had been his eyes.

She knew those eyes, had stared into them recently, though she couldn't place where . . .

"I apologize, Miss Webster, for the inconvenience. But I will need you to come with me once we exit the elevator."

She stared, blinked, her heart suddenly fluttering as she put the whole picture together. The earring, the dreadlocks, the eyes she'd stared into last night in the taxi's rearview mirror.

This was the man who was after Kelly John. The man whose job it was to take others' lives.

"Come with you where? Why?" The last word was no more than a whispered squeak. Talking was impossible when she couldn't even breathe.

"I'm sure you understand that I cannot stop for explanations at the moment, but you and I will have plenty of time to chat soon enough."

She said nothing, thinking of her cell in her purse, the building's security officer in the lobby, the emergency call phone in the control panel, which she could use if she could disable him somehow.

She wanted to laugh at herself for even considering the thought. His lilting accent was the only thing about him that was soft. The rest of him was lean and hard, weathered and scarred, and very, very frightening.

She shifted the strap of her purse more securely onto her shoulder and lifted her chin. "I'm assuming I don't have a choice?"

"If I don't return with you to my employer within"—he glanced at the multi-dial face of the watch wrapped around his wrist with a wide leather band—"eight minutes, he will be on his way to retrieve what your Mr. Beach took from us. The retrieval will go much more smoothly with you tucked safely away."

"Blackmail."

"Exactly, though you shouldn't look on it in a negative light."

"Why not?"

"You'll be able to discover your lover's true colors. Will he choose you, or betray the trust of those counting on him to uphold the law?"

Twelve

It wasn't until Hank's stomach sent up a loud mournful howl complaining of hunger that he realized his lunch hour had come and gone some ninety minutes past.

He'd been caught up on the World Wide Web, checking into the—what was the word for fancy knickknacks and extras?—accoutrements he was thinking of having installed in Maddy Bar None's new training barn, and hadn't paid mind to the time.

Deciding no horse really needed a designer saddle blanket and anyone who thought such needed to be shot, he reached across his desk for the phone and punched the intercom button.

"Emma? You want to order me up a sandwich and have Brighton's bring it over?" He waited for a moment, shutting down his browser windows, and when he got no response, tried again. "Emma?"

This time he decided she must have stepped away for a necessary break. Hell, he needed one, too. Forget having Brighton's deliver his lunch. The walk down the block would do him good.

Too much office air was drying out his brain. Too much sitting on his backside, which was spreading like bad weeds, instead of working in the field with his boys on SG-5's jobs.

Not to mention too much time spent surfing the Web. And why the hell they called it surfing was beyond him, unless it was from the way it sucked a man down and tried to drown him in more information than he could swallow in a lifetime.

Pushing out of his chair and rounding his desk, he crossed the office, thinking of swallowing a big juicy roast beef on rye instead. Good ol' thick onions and cheddar cheese. Lots of horseradish mayo.

At least that was what he was thinking until he pulled open the door, found Emma's desk still empty, and a man sitting alone on her visitor's sofa, an ankle squared up over the opposite knee, the *Wall Street Journal* spread open on his lap.

He glanced up over the rims of his wire-framed glasses, folded the paper upon seeing Hank, and got to his feet. "Mr. Smithson, I presume?"

"Who's inquiring?" Hank asked, slipping in behind Emma's desk should he need to hit the alarm button beneath her desk that would ring on the twenty-fourth floor. Something about the man's look set off a bell.

"My name is Oliver Shore. I recently assisted an associate of yours, a Mr. Shaughnessey? During a siege at the sandwich shop to which I believe you're headed?"

He inclined his head toward Emma's speaker phone, and Hank felt as if he'd never be able to swallow anything again because of the hatred balled up like a cancer in his throat.

This man was Spectra IT.

Hank braced a hand on the corner of Emma's desk momentarily, using his thumb to hit the button hidden deep in the wooden lip. "I suppose we should step into my office."

Oliver Shore nodded, indicating that Hank should go ahead before lacing his hands at his back. Hank stopped inside the doorway, closing it once the other man had entered.

The chess game was on.

Hank walked to his desk, not bothering to offer a seat to the other man—though he took one anyway—and not bothering to sit in his own. Instead, he stood to face the enemy.

"You've got two minutes." It would take less for his boys upstairs to show.

"I think your assistant's well-being might be worth more than two minutes."

It took a moment for the words' meaning to settle, then . . . Emma!

Sonofabitch!

Hank reached into his desktop humidor, his heart thumping in his chest as hard as it had when he'd learned of his Madelyn's breast cancer.

He held the cigar by both ends, rolled it in his fingers, took a long minute before looking up. "Where is she?"

"She's quite safe, and will be able to return to her duties in the morning." Shore paused, crossed his legs, and leaned back in the chair. "As long as I get what I want tonight."

Hank's office door opened then, Christian Bane walking into the office along with Mick Savin and Tripp Shaughnessey. All Tripp needed was one look at Hank's visitor and his face turned a mighty beet red.

Shore used his grip on the chair's arms and pushed to his feet, his gaze traveling from one man to the next and settling finally on Tripp. "Mr. Shaughnessey. A pleasure to see you again."

"No. It's not," was all Tripp said, his arms crossed over his chest, his stance shoulder-wide. "What do you want?"

Shore removed his glasses, retrieved his handkerchief to clean the lenses, spoke while staring at the motion of his hands. "I was just about to explain to Mr. Smithson that I believe one of your associates is holding an item belonging to me. Until it is returned, I will be holding onto an item belonging to him."

"What's the item?" Christian demanded, cutting to the chase, his gaze grabbing hard to Hank's.

The Montecristo Corona Grande crumbled to the desktop. "He's got Emma."

Emma sat in the straight-backed chair with her back straight, her hands clutching her purse in her lap. Across the unremarkable table in the unremarkable room that seemed suited for interrogations sat her abductor.

He slouched back on his spine, legs spread beneath the table, hands laced behind his head, biceps sharply defined. He'd hooked his sunglasses in the neckline of his black T-shirt, and with his long thick dreads held back by an olive green bandana, his face was completely visible.

Unfortunately, it was also completely unreadable.

She'd hoped to be able to find something, anything, in his expression that would clue her in as to what was going to happen, because she seriously doubted she'd be released as promised at the end of the day.

"How long am I going to have to sit here?" she finally asked because the tense silence was working her nerves as intended.

His dark eyes twinkled, a response as enigmatic as all his others had been. "Do not feel that you must sit. The room is not large, but the length should be enough for you to pace."

She thought of the click-click-click of her heels on the tiled floor, wondered how long the echo would take to drive him mad.

Then the subtle implication of his suggestion set in. "Why would I need to pace when you've assured me I have nothing to worry about?"

His shrug was more a flex of muscle then a lift of his shoulders. "I was thinking of you expending nervous energy. Surely you found pacing effective during your previous eight-month confinement."

Her heart skittered in her chest. "You know about my going to jail?"

"I do," he admitted with a nod. "And I know the experience will make this one seem like nothing."

He said it almost as if delivering a compliment. "Trust me. This isn't going to seem like nothing. That will never happen."

He dropped his hands from behind his head to cross his arms over his chest as he considered her. "You sound so certain."

"I am." Why would he think otherwise? Two heartbeats counted off two seconds, and she pushed her chair back, the feet sliding cleanly, almost silently, over the floor's gleaming white tiles.

Then again, he'd been the one so sure that she needed to pace, and here she was—the thing of it being that her worries were more about what this man and the group he worked for had planned for Kelly John.

God, three hours ago she'd been on her way home to make him waffles. And now her stomach was heaving with the possibilities of what was happening to him. If worrying about her was going to be his downfall.

No. That wasn't going to happen. She refused to believe it. She'd proven to him that she was capable and competent; surely she had.

"I missed lunch, you know," she said, standing behind her captor now, staring at the back of his head, at his dreadlocks hanging between his shoulders.

Thinking she might be able to wrap his hair around his neck and choke him, gain her freedom . . . through the door that had no handle on the inside. "I don't suppose food's a possibility, though, is it?"

"If you were truly hungry, I could arrange it."

She stuck out her tongue at the back of his head, wondering too late if he had eyeballs there. Wondering, as well, if she should be more panicked than she actually was.

She didn't know why she wasn't more worried except that she trusted Kelly John, Hank, and the others implicitly. Trusted them to know the right thing to do. Trusted them to get her out of here.

Trusted them with her life.

Her chin came up as that reality settled around her, comforting her, cocooning her. Knowing no more than she did, she didn't doubt for a moment that she'd be out of here long before it was time for dinner.

Or before this man received orders to dispose of any loose ends left alive.

She gulped once and returned to her chair, pushed her purse to the side, and laced her fingers together on the table. Leaning forward, she met his curious gaze. "I'm not sure why or how you know so much about me, but knowing nothing about you, I feel at a disadvantage."

He looked at her for a long minute, then simply laughed. "And what would you like to know?"

As if he'd really tell her. As if he cared that she didn't like his holding the upper hand. "This organization you work for? What exactly is it that you do for them?"

"Are you sure that's what you want to know?"

No, she wasn't. She wasn't at all. "Sure. Why not?"

"Because I don't know how it could help your state of mind to learn that I am a hired killer."

Thirteen

The jungle smelled of things dank and oozing and rotten in ways Kelly John hated to contemplate.

It wasn't the sort of ripe that was about a nice sweet peach, but about half-empty beer cans left for three weeks in the sealed cooler of a pickup truck parked in the sun.

And it was especially unappetizing considering he had his nose buried in the mud, his eyes and mouth closed, his stomach churning as he waited for the Nicaraguan guerillas ahead to disappear into the thick canopy of foliage.

Yeah, the waiting sucked and the ground smelled like shit. But it would be really bad form to get caught taking out the underground lab operated by the cartel from whom he bought his blow—blow he used to pay off informants and bribe cokeheads willing to sell out their countrymen for a line.

Such was the way of the drug trade. One often took a fat step back for every two tiptoed forward. The trick was to keep the endgame in sight. A trick that didn't always make it easy to rise above the scum, but it helped.

Especially on the days when the green stuff seeped from the eyes he saw in the mirror as thickly as from those beaded in the faces of the dealers topping his hit list.

Then there was this particular mission, which was about more than the destruction of Rubén Bolano's distribution center. It was life or death to Kelly John's squad and their successful record of slamming the brakes on the Nicaraguan drug traffic.

And at least he wasn't alone. Jeremy lay on one side, Bill on the other, Eric and Sasha a meter to the east, Randy a meter to the west. The Six Shooters, as the detail had come to be known.

A detail that was going to be down to five as a result of this op and one big fat mouth. It had been discussed and decided. This was the only way out. And he would act as trigger man.

Lifting his head enough to open his eyes, he held his breath and peered through the moss draped from his helmet like off the branch of a tree. The coast was clear.

He raised one hand and signaled. The detail scrambled up to their knees, moved forward in absolute silence. Birds continued to chirp overhead, insects to swarm and buzz.

The nearest trap door into the lab was on the jungle floor ten meters north, the second ten meters farther. He waved Bill, Sasha, and Eric on ahead, slowing as Randy made his way closer, flanking Kelly John's other side.

He glanced briefly at Jeremy, who set his jaw and nodded. The time had come. Bellies to the ground, the trio slithered forward, Kelly John dropping back slowly, sweat pooling at the base of his spine.

His mind raced, whipping through a list of other so-

*lutions. Not a one of them stuck. He couldn't believe
things had come to this, but what the fuck was he supposed to do?*

*His methods of taking care of business fell outside
the law. Of course they did. That was how things here
were done. And he sure as hell wasn't going to risk the
lives and futures of four of the best men he'd ever
known because of one with a god complex.*

*Randy had to be eliminated before he did more
damage than he'd already done, talking out of turn
when the code demanded silence, demanded loyalty.
Demanded trust. They couldn't be six men acting as
one when one wanted all the glory.*

*That one had slipped past Kelly John, crawling for-
ward on his belly, using only his elbows and knees.
Kelly John closed his eyes, curled his fingers around
the garrote he'd taken off one of Bolano's men. If he
went down for this, so be it. He'd be saving more lives
than the one he was taking.*

*And, at that, he dashed off the quickest prayer for
forgiveness that he could . . .*

Kelly John stood staring out the window of Hank's office, smelling his own fear instead of the sweetness of Emma,
watching the movement of traffic on the street below, yet
seeing only her face as she'd so carefully pulled closed the
bedroom door this morning.

He should've gotten up, dressed, and come with her into
the office instead of lying in her bed all day like a lazy sex
slug, thinking he'd just stay there until she got home and
got naked again. Or so had been the plan until the phone
call four hours later.

Since then, he'd been pacing the ops center, working his
contacts, queuing the last few hours of the building's security tapes, canvassing the neighborhood, certain Emma was

being held close. He'd seen her enter just before eight-thirty this morning, but found no evidence of her exit, her abductor, or even Oliver Shore.

He should've been with her. He should've kept her in his sights. He should've known the night had been too good to be real. Having Emma snatched away was a cruel punishment being wrongly meted out.

She shouldn't have to pay for her belief in him. She shouldn't be the one atoning for his sins. He'd screwed up, and gone on to make it worse by bringing her into a dangerous situation. Apparently, he was beyond learning his lesson, and the cost this time was astronomical.

The woman he loved was out there waiting for a garrote he wasn't sure he'd be able to slip from her neck in time. He slammed his fist into the top of Hank's credenza. He'd left the lights off, and it was dark here.

He'd told himself he needed the blackness to think, to process what was happening, to sort out and coordinate what steps to take next. The reality was that he needed a minute to hide while his eyes dried and the thick ball of grief in his throat subsided.

God, he loved her. He loved her. What the flying fuck was he going to do if he'd lost her already? He cracked his knuckles against the wall this time, welcoming the pain because it made him remember that he was alive, that she was alive, and tears were not doing anyone any good.

He flinched then, feeling Hank's hand come down on his shoulder. The older man squeezed the tight muscles. "We'll get her back, son. We'll get her back."

All Kelly John could do was nod. And, at that, he dashed off the quickest prayer for forgiveness that he could . . .

Kelly John stood on the empty fifth floor of the parking garage adjacent to the building housing Smithson Engineering, shifting his weight restlessly from foot to foot, his hands in his pockets, his head up, his ears pricked.

Except for the camouflage and grease paint, he looked much as he had that day in Nicaragua, wearing boots, fatigues, and a desperate sense of despair.

Hank stood nearby, the two of them waiting near the pillar closest to the elevator, as instructed by Oliver Shore, alone and unarmed and in possession of the USB flash drive Kelly John had taken from Marian Diamonds less than forty-eight hours before.

Tripp was the one with the weapon. The one Kelly John *wanted* handling a weapon. The only one whose detailed history before the Smithson Group he was privy to. Though even knowing the extent of Tripp's sniper skills didn't do much to ease the tension of being at the mercy of Spectra IT.

He didn't even realize he'd started pacing until Hank stepped into his path, took hold of his shoulders and stopped him. "Wearing a groove in the floor isn't going to get her here any faster, son."

He knew that. He knew that. What worried him was whether she was going to get here at all. He didn't put a lot of trust in the words of the crime syndicate who'd caged Christian Bane in the jungles of Thailand and left him to die.

"We shouldn't have asked her to do this." He shook his head. "Not something involving Spectra. It wasn't smart. It was too risky. Too dangerous—"

Hank cut him off with a thick finger stabbed into the center of his chest. "Your ass was on the line. It was all we could come up with having no more notice than we did."

Kelly John shoved his hands to his hips, stared off into the dark corner behind the garage's elevator, breathed in the musty scents of exhaust and dirty concrete. "And the tapes didn't even work. We didn't prove anything. What a fucking waste of time."

"Rein it in, son. Rein it in." Hank leaned back against the support pillar. "We didn't get the chance to use them. You know that."

That was what was killing him. That he'd put Emma in harm's way for nothing. A burst of sick laughter tore through his chest. He scratched there, working at the ache. "Hell, it was a joke to think we could pull it off. A fucking goddamn joke."

"Oh, I don't know, Mr. Beach."

At the sound of Oliver Shore's voice, Hank looked up. Kelly John whirled around. Both men watched the other's soundless approach.

"It was quite an inventive exercise at throwing us off your track." Shore continued forward, his steps silent. "Had I not had experience with Mr. Shaughnessey, I might have been unaware of your interest in our diamond trade."

Kelly John didn't give a shit about diamonds. "Where's Emma?"

"Soon, Mr. Beach. Soon." Shore stopped a good two meters back. "First, however, please have your man put down his weapon."

Hank raised his hand to signal Tripp. Kelly John cursed under his breath. "It's done. Where's Emma?"

Adjusting the fit of his glasses on his ears, Shore shook his head. "I'm not sure if your impatience is admirable or annoying, Mr. Beach. But rest assured that we can complete our transaction as soon as you produce what I've come for."

"Let me see her first," Kelly John said stalling for time.

"Quite simply, no." Shore held out one hand, gestured with his fingers, the smile on his face as false as the aura of SG-5's compliant cooperation. "I have no intention of losing what advantage I might have."

Shit. *Shit, shit, shit.* Kelly John dug the flash drive from his fatigue's pocket and slapped it into the other man's hand. Shore turned the storage device over in his palm, studying both sides.

Kelly John ground his jaw and hoped he got a chance to plead his case. How the hell could he have known he'd need to trade the drive for Emma?

Gesturing with the gadget, Shore met Kelly John's gaze from over the rims of his glasses. "Of course the fact that you've viewed the data stored on the drive means our deal is off."

"Viewed once." *Good evening, Mr. Beach. This drive will self-destruct the first time you plug it in and open the files, rendering it pretty fucking useless as a bargaining tool.* "Not copied. Not transferred. Not stored. Not memorized."

Shore chuckled cruelly. "And I'm to trust that you're telling me the truth?"

Hank stepped up. "You can trust both of us. We're telling you the goddamned truth."

"Perhaps." Shore's fist closed around the device. "But I prefer to trust my instincts telling me you're not."

"What the hell does that mean?" Kelly John fairly growled.

"It means that you can keep the flash drive"—he offered to return it—"and I'll keep Miss Webster."

Kelly John grabbed the storage device and skipped it across the garage floor like a stone. It hit the ramp's barrier and splintered. "Let her go. Take me instead. Do what you want to with me. Just let Emma go."

The tension in the garage raged around them unchecked. He was burning from the inside out, flames of hatred, flames of fear. He wanted to crush this man's skull only slightly less than he wanted to fall to his knees and beg for Emma's release.

"No, I don't think I will," Shore said, having clearly never considered the option.

"Wait, Shore," Hank ordered.

But the other man had already began walking away. "I don't deal only in diamonds, you know. I know of a market hungry for pretty white girls. Especially those with the legs and tits of this one."

Two seconds later, he stopped. His body jerked once, convulsed, then hit the ground. A pool of red blossomed from the bullet hole centered between his eyes.

Kelly John's heart exploded. "Tripp! No!"

"It wasn't me, man! I swear. It wasn't me," Tripp yelled. A Weatherby Tactical TRR slung over his shoulder, he dropped from the overhead cross beam to a crouch on the floor, pushed up and jogged over to where Hank stood staring down at the dead Spectra agent. "K.J., I swear. That's not my bullet."

Kelly John fell to his knees, sat back on his heels, dragged his hands down his face, and howled as his guts turned inside out. "Emma!"

What the ever-lovin' hell had just happened? If Tripp wasn't the shooter . . . oh God, Emma. Emma!

No, this wasn't real. How could this be real? How could his only connection to Emma be dead at his feet? Breathe, breathe. *Breathe!* He pitched forward, dropped his forehead to the ground, heard Hank and Tripp move closer.

He didn't want them closer. He needed room. He had to get up, find her. Find her. She had to be close. He hadn't yet talked to the Smithson staff or the rest of the building's tenants. Yeah, that was the plan.

A plan that sucked ass since his body was now made of lead.

At least he was breathing. His chest might not know it, might ache as if still needing oxygen, but he could hear the air wheeze in and out of his lungs. And then, moments later, another sound permeated his brain. The sound of footsteps.

"Holy hell," Hank gasped.

"Awesome," Tripp shouted.

Kelly John looked up. Managed to croak out, "Emma?"

And then he was on his feet, staggering forward, and she was in his arms, and nothing in the world had ever felt this good, this right, this perfect.

He touched every part of her he could find, assuring himself that she was real and alive and unharmed. "Oh, baby. I can't believe you're here. What happened? Where did you come from? Where have you been?"

She shook her head, her cheeks damp on his chest. "I don't know. He just let me go."

"Who let you go?" he demanded. He was going to get the fucker. "Who was it?"

"The taxi driver. From last night. He told me to give you this." She pulled away. And when he held out his hand, she dropped an earring into his palm.

A single diamond stud.

Sonofabitch! Julian's Spectra assassin. "He's the one who took you? When? Where?"

"In the elevator. When I left for lunch, he was there." She shuddered, drew in a deep breath, cuddled back up into his body. "He took me into the basement, through a subway maintenance tunnel, and up a flight of stairs into another building."

He wrapped his arms around her, held her tighter than he'd known he could hold a woman. "Did he hurt you? Did he touch you?"

She shook her head. "No. In fact, he said he would feed me if I was hungry. But he knew that I wasn't. That I wouldn't be able to eat."

He cupped the back of her head with one hand, cradled her close to his chest with the other, swore he would never let her out of his sight, would never let her go. "God, Emma. I thought I was going mad. The thought of losing you . . ."

"Me, too." She sighed. "I knew you'd find me, though."

"Yeah? How's that?"

"I trusted you to."

"Crazy woman."

"No. A woman in love."

He rolled his eyes because he was so mad for her. So wild with having her here in his arms. "Here we go with that war thing again."

"Hmm. You're not running this time."

He shook his head. "Too much trouble. It's easier just to love you."

"You love me?" she asked breathlessly.

He nodded. "I do."

"Wow." She pulled back, looked up into his eyes. "Those two words must've scared you."

"In the past, maybe." He leaned down, nuzzled his cheek to hers. "Not now with Mata Hari watching my back."

Meet the men of the Smithson Group—five spies whose best work is done in the field and between the sheets. Smart, built, trained to do everything well—and that's everything—they're the guys you want on your side of the bed. Go deep undercover? No problem. Take out the bad guys? Done. Play by the rules? I don't think so. Indulge a woman's every fantasy? Happy to please, ma'am. Fall in love? Hey, even a secret agent's got his weak spots . . .

Bad boys. Good spies. Unforgettable lovers.

Episode One:
THE BANE AFFAIR
by
Alison Kent

"Smart, funny, exciting, touching, and *hot*."
—Cherry Adair

"Fast, dangerous, sexy."—Shannon McKenna

<u>Get started with Christian Bane, SG–5</u>

Christian Bane is a man of few words, so when he talks, people listen. One of the Smithson Group's elite force, Christian's also the walking wounded, haunted by his past. Something about being betrayed by a woman, then left to die in a Thai prison by the notorious crime syndicate Spectra IT gives a guy demons. But now, Spectra has made a secret deal with a top scientist to crack a governmental encryption technology, and Christian has his orders: Pose as Spectra boss Peter Deacon. Going deep undercover as the slick womanizer will be tough for Christian. Getting cozy with the scientist's beautiful goddaughter, Natasha, to get information won't be. But the closer he gets to Natasha, the harder it gets to deceive her. She's so alluring, so trusting, so completely unexpected he suspects someone's been giving out faulty intel. If Natasha isn't the criminal he was led to believe, they're both being played for fools. Now, with Spectra closing in, Christian's best chance for survival is to confront his demons and trust the only one he can . . . Natasha.

Available from Brava in October 2004.

Episode Two:
THE SHAUGHNESSEY ACCORD
by
Alison Kent

Get hot and bothered with Tripp Shaughnessey, SG–5

When someone screams Tripp Shaughnessey's name, it's usually a woman in the throes of passion or one who's just caught him with his hand in the proverbial cookie jar. Sometimes it's both. Tripp is sarcastic, fun-loving, and funny, with a habit of seducing every woman he says hello to. But the one who really gets him hot and bothered is Glory Brighton, the curvaceous owner of his favorite sandwich shop. The nonstop banter between Glory and Tripp has been leading up to a full-body kiss in the back storeroom. And that's just where they are when all hell breaks loose. Glory's past includes some very bad men connected to Spectra, men convinced she may have important intel hidden in her place. Now, with the shop under siege, and gunmen holding customers hostage, Tripp shows Glory his true colors: He's no sweet, rumpled "engineer" from the Smithson Group, but a well-trained, hard-core covert op whose easygoing rep is about to be put to the test . . .

Available from Brava in November 2004.

Episode Three:
THE SAMMS AGENDA
by
Alison Kent

Get down and dirty with Julian Samms, SG–5

From his piercing blue eyes to his commanding presence, everything about Julian Samms says all-business and no bull. He expects a lot from his team—some say too much. But that's how you keep people alive, by running things smooth, clean, and quick. Under Julian's watch, that's how it plays. Except today. The mission was straightforward: Extract Katrina Flurry, ex-girlfriend of deposed Spectra frontman Peter Deacon, from her Miami condo before a hit man can silence her for good. But things didn't go according to plan, and Julian's suddenly on the run with a woman who gives new meaning to high maintenance. Stuck in a cheap motel with a force of nature who seems determined to get them killed, Julian can't believe his luck. Katrina is infuriating, unpredictable, adorable, and possibly the most exciting, sexy woman he's ever met. A woman who makes Julian want to forget his playbook and go wild, spending hours in bed. And on the off-chance that they don't get out alive, Julian's new live-for-today motto is starting right now . . .

Available from Brava in December 2004.

Episode Four:
THE BEACH ALIBI
by
Alison Kent

Get deep undercover with Kelly John Beach, SG–5

Kelly John Beach is the go-to guy known for covering all the bases and moving in the shadows like a ghost. But now, the ultimate spy is in big trouble: during his last mission, he was caught breaking into a Spectra IT high-rise on one of their video surveillance cameras. The SG–5 team has to make an alternate tape fast, one that proves K.J. was elsewhere at the time of the break-in. The plan is simple: Someone from Smithson will pose as K.J.'s lover, and SG–5's strategically placed cameras will record their every intimate, erotic encounter in elevators, theater hallways, and other daring forums. But Kelly John never expects that "alibi" to come in the form of Emma Webster, the sexy coworker who has starred in so many of his not-for-prime-time fantasies. Getting his hands—and anything else he can—on Emma under the guise of work is a dream come true. Deceiving the good-hearted, trusting woman isn't. And when Spectra realizes that the way to K.J. is through Emma, the spy is ready to come in from the cold, and show her how far he'll go to protect the woman he loves . . .

Available from Brava in January 2005.

Episode Five:
THE MCKENZIE ARTIFACT
by
Alison Kent

Get what you came for with Eli McKenzie, SG–5

Five months ago, SG–5 operative Eli McKenzie was in deep cover in Mexico, infiltrating a Spectra ring that kidnaps young girls and sells them into a life beyond imagining. Not being able to move on the Spectra scum right away was torture for the tough-but-compassionate superspy. But that wasn't the only problem—someone on the inside was slowly poisoning Eli, clouding his judgment and forcing him to make an abrupt trip back to the Smithson Group's headquarters to heal. Now, Eli's ready to return . . . with a vengeance. It seems his quick departure left a private investigator named Stella Banks in some hot water. Spectra operatives have nabbed the nosy Stella and are awaiting word on how to handle her disposal. Eli knows the only way to save her life and his is to reveal himself to Stella and get her to trust him. Seeing the way Stella takes care of the frightened girls melts Eli's armor, and soon, they find that the best way to survive this brutal assignment is to steal time in each other's arms. It's a bliss Eli's intent on keeping, no matter what he has to do to protect it. Because Eli McKenzie has unfinished business with Spectra—and with the woman who has renewed his heart—this is one man who always finishes what he starts . . .

Available from Brava in February 2005.

Please sample other books
in this wonderful series:
Available right now—
THE BANE AFFAIR

Christian watched the road rush by beneath the car, the roar in his ears much more than that of the engine or the tires. He should have trusted his instincts earlier. Susan's turning green wasn't about the amount of alcohol left in her system at all.

He held out his right hand, gripped the steering wheel with his left. "Hand me your phone."

"Why?"

"The phone, Natasha." He didn't have time to argue. Didn't have time to explain. Had time to do nothing but react. An exit loomed to the right. He downshifted to slow the car and swerved across two lanes to take it. Ahead and behind, the road was blessedly free of traffic. "The phone, now, please."

"I don't think so," she said, yelping when he reached across and grabbed it out of her hand.

She slumped defiantly into her seat, arms crossed over her chest. Checking again for oncoming vehicles, he pried open the phone and removed the battery, tossed the case over the top of the car toward the ditch, the power supply to the side of the road a quarter mile away.

"What the hell are you doing?" she screamed, whirling

on him, fists flying, nails raking, grabbing for the steering wheel.

He hit the brakes, whipped into the skid. The fast stop and shoulder strap slammed her back into the bucket. He kept her there with the barrel of the Ruger .45-caliber he snatched from beneath his seat. "Sit down. Nothing's going to happen to you if you sit down and be still."

She didn't say a word, but he heard her hyperventilating panic above the roar in his ears.

"Calm down, Natasha. Listen to me. No one's going to get hurt." His pulse pounded. His mind whirred. "I just need you to be still and be quiet."

"You're pointing a gun at me and you want me to be still and be quiet? You fucking piece of shit." She swiped back the hair from her face. "Don't tell me to be still and be quiet. In fact, don't tell me anything at all. When Susan doesn't hear from me later, she's calling the cops. She knows exactly where we are and what we're driving. So whatever the hell you think you're doing here, you're not getting away with it. You lying, fucking bastard."

He caught her gaze, saw the glassy fear, the damp tears she wouldn't shed, the delineated vessels in the whites of her eyes like a road map penned in red. He wanted to tell her the truth, that he was one of the good guys, to reassure her that she could trust him, that no harm would come her way—but he couldn't tell her any of that and he refused to compound his sins with yet another lie.

And so he issued a growling order. "Shut the hell up, Natasha. Now."

Grabbing his phone from his belt, he punched in a preset code. The phone rang once. Julian Samms picked up the other end. "Shoot."

"I need to get to the farm. Where's Briggs?"

"Hang," Julian ordered, and Christian waited while his SG-5 partner contacted Hank's chopper pilot, waited and watched Natasha hug herself with shaking hands, tears finally and silently rolling down her cheeks.

"I've got you on GPS. Briggs can be there in thirty, but you need to bank the car. And he needs a place to land. Hang."

More waiting. More looking for approaching cars. More watching Natasha glare, shake, and cry.

Christian switched from handset to earphone and lowered the gun to his thigh, keeping his gaze on Natasha while waiting for Julian's instructions. She seemed so small, so wounded, and he kicked himself all over again for failing to make it clear that their involvement was purely physical.

He should have spelled that out from day one, made it more clear that Peter Deacon took trophies, not lovers. But he'd never given her any such warning. Not that it would've done any good. Hell, he knew the lay of the land and here he was, so tied up in knots over what he was putting her through that he couldn't even think straight.

"My name is Christian Bane," he finally said, owing her that much. "That's all I can tell you right now."

She snorted, flipped him the bird, and turned to stare out her window.

"Bane."

"Yeah." Hand to his earpiece, he turned his attention back to Julian.

"Two miles ahead on the right," Julian said as Christian shifted into gear and accelerated, "there's a cutoff. Through a gate. Looks like a dirt road, rutted as hell."

He brought the car up to speed, scanned the landscape. "Got it," he said, and made the turn, nearly bottoming out on the first bump.

"Half a mile, make another right. Other side of a stand of trees."

"Almost there." He reached the cutoff and turned again, caught sight of the tumbledown barn and stables, the flat pasture beyond. Perfect. Plenty of room for the chopper and cover for the car. "Tell Briggs we're waiting."

A short couple of seconds, and Julian said, "He says make it twenty. K.J.'s with him. He'll bring back the car. I'll keep the line open. Hank's expecting you."

"Thanks, J."

Christian maneuvered the Ferrari down the road that wasn't much more than a trail of flattened grass leading to a clearing surrounding the barn. Once he'd circled behind it, he tugged the wire from his ear, cut the engine, and pocketed the keys. When he opened his door, Natasha finally looked over.

"Going someplace?" she asked snidely.

"We both are," he bit back. "Get out."

"You can go to hell, but I'm not going anywhere."

"Actually, you are. And you're going with me." He reminded her that he was the one with the gun.

She got out of the car, slammed the door, and was off like a rocket back down the road. Shit, shit, shit. He checked the safety, shoved the Ruger into his waistband next to the SIG, and took off after her. She was fast, but he was faster. He closed in, but she never slowed, leaving him no choice.

He grabbed her arm. She spun toward him. He took her to the ground, bracing himself for the blow. He landed hard on his shoulder, doing what he could to cushion her fall. She grunted at the impact, and he rolled on top of her, pinning her to the ground with his weight and his strength.

Her adrenaline made for a formidable foe. She shoved at his chest, pummeled him with her fists when he refused to move. He finally had no choice but to grab her wrists, stretch out her arms above her head, hold her there.

Rocks and dirt and twigs bit into his fingers. He knew she felt the bite in the backs of her hands, but still he straddled her, capturing her legs between his.

"You want to wait like this? Twenty minutes? Because we can." His chest heaved in sync with the rapid rise and fall of hers. "Or we can get up and wait at the car. I'm good either way. You tell me."

"Get off me." She spat out the words.

He rolled up and away, kept his hands on her wrists and pulled her to her feet. Then he tugged her close, making sure he had her full attention, ignoring the stabbing pain in his shoulder that didn't hurt half as much as the one in his gut. "I'm not going to put up with any shit here, Natasha. Both of our lives are very likely in danger."

"Oh, right. I can see that. You being the one with the gun and all." She jerked her hands from his.

He let her go, walking a few feet behind her as she made her way slowly back to the barn and the parked car. She had nowhere to run; hopefully, he'd made his point. He had no intention to harm her, no *reason* to harm her, but he needed to finish this job, to make sure Spectra didn't get their hands on whatever it was Bow had to sell.

And now that he'd been stupid enough to get his cover blown . . .

"Where are you taking me?" She splayed shaking palms over the Ferrari's engine bay, staring down at her skin, which was ghostly pale against the car's black sheen.

"To get the answers you've been asking for," he said, guilt eating him from the inside out, and looked up with no small bit of relief at the *thwup-thwup-thwup* of an approaching chopper.

And also available from Brava—

THE SHAUGHNESSEY ACCORD

Tripp grabbed Glory by the shoulders, twirled her bodily across the room and into a tight corner where two of the shelving units met at a right angle.

"I know this part," she whispered as he wedged her inside. "Stay put."

He nodded, drew his gun and pressed his back to the wall at her side. The door slammed open and bounced off the cinderblocks behind. Tripp held the weapon raised, both hands at the ready, his heart doing a freight train run in his chest.

Beside him, Glory barely breathed. The shelf of supplies to his right blocked his view of the door but didn't keep his nostrils from flaring, his neck hairs from bristling, his adrenaline from pumping like gasoline.

He sensed their visitor long before the black-garbed man swung around and aimed his gun straight at Glory's head. The intruder stepped over his own downed associate and held out a gloved hand.

"Give me the gun and she will not die."

Tripp cursed violently under his breath, weighing his options on a different scale than he would've used in this situation had Glory not been involved.

If he'd had time to do more than react, time to think,

plot and plan, he would've stashed the gun behind a can of olives and used the butt end to up his own prisoner count when the time was right.

Instead, he found himself surrendering the very piece that would've gone a long way to protecting Glory from this thug. But he was stuck using nothing but the wits that never seemed to operate at full throttle unless he had a contingency plan.

Right now all he had was a gut full of bile. That and a big fat regret that he didn't think better on his feet than he did.

Having passed over the gun, he raised both hands, palms out. "Let's neither of us go off half-cocked here."

The other man considered him for a long, strange moment, his black eyes broadcasting zero emotion while he stared for what seemed like forever before he tugged the ski mask from his head.

He was young. Tripp would've guessed twenty-three, twenty-four. Except when he looked at the kid's eyes. His expression was so dark, so blank, so unfeeling that it was like looking at a long-dead corpse.

Without moving his gaze from Tripp's, the kid shouted sharp orders in Vietnamese. Two other similarly garbed goons entered the storeroom and dragged away the dead weight Tripp had left in the middle of the floor.

Once the cast of extras was gone, the lead player planted his feet and shifted his gaze between Tripp and Glory, both hands hanging at his sides, one worrying the ski mask into a black fabric ball, the other flexed and ready and holding the gun.

"An interesting situation we find ourselves in here, isn't it?" he finally asked. "Miss Brighton, would you introduce me to your friend?"

"What do you want?" she asked before Tripp could stop her. "Tell me what you want. I'll give it to you, and you can get out of my shop."

His black hair fell over his brow. "If what I have come for was so easily obtained, then I would have it in my possession by now."

He was after whatever the courier from the diamond exchange had delivered to the Spectra agent. Tripp was sure of it. Was sure as well the information would detail future packets removed from Sierra Leone.

The ski mask fell to the floor. "I'm waiting, Miss Brighton."

"He's a friend. A customer." Her hands fluttered at her waist. "We're just . . . good friends."

"You allow all your customers to visit your storeroom?" His mouth twisted cruelly. "Or only the ones with whom you are intimate?"

Glory gasped. Tripp placed his arm in front of her, a protective barrier he knew did little good. "C'mon, man. There's no need to go there."

The Asian kid raised a brow. "Actually, I think there is. Getting what I want often requires me to explore a defense's most vulnerable link. It is not always pleasant, but it can be quite effective."

Tripp was pissed and rapidly getting more so. "Well, there are no links here to explore. So do as the lady suggested. Take what you've come for and let us all get back to our lives."

"Were it only so simple," he said as he gestured Glory forward. She forced her way past the barricade of Tripp's arm. "But we seem to have hit what will no doubt be an endlessly long impasse thanks to one of Miss Brighton's customers."

Glory looked from the kid back to Tripp, her eyes asking questions to which he had zero answers. "I don't understand."

"You are very predictable, Miss Brighton. As is your customer base. Same sandwiches. Same lunch hours. That made planning this job quite easy. I'm assuming the courier using your place of business for a drop point found your tight schedule advantageous, too."

Tripp's mind raced like the wind. The kid was talking way too much. His gang had blacked out the shop's single security camera, had made entry without alerting anyone to their presence, had secured the scene and done it all while Tripp made love to Glory.

Trip had been monitoring the shop for weeks and he'd never noticed the shop being scouted. He hadn't been wise to the intrusion until the kid had shot the lock off the door.

A guy who followed through on such flawless planning didn't start yapping his flap unless he felt there would be no survivors but him. And Tripp had a feeling they were looking into the dead eyes of an animal who'd fight to the death before being taken alive.

Here's a preview of

THE SAMMS AGENDA

South Miami, Friday, 3:30 P.M.

Julian hit the ground with a jolt, seams ripping, bones crunching, joints popping as he rolled to his feet and came up into a full-throttle run.

Coattails flying, he sprinted across the pool's cement deck, hurdled the shattered planter, and gave Katrina no chance to do more than gasp as he grabbed her upper arm and ran.

"Go! Go! Go! Go! Go!"

He propelled her forward, knowing he could run a hell of a lot faster then she could, the both of them dragged down even more by the *slap, slap, slap* of her ridiculous shoes.

She seemed to reach the very same conclusion at the very same time, however, and kicked off the slides to run in bare feet.

Once across the deck and up the courtyard stairs, he shoved open the enclosure's gate. Another bullet ricocheted off the iron railing.

Katrina screamed, but kept up with the pace he set as they pushed through and barreled down the arched walkway toward the parking garage.

Her Lexus was closer, but he doubted she had her keys and didn't have time to stop, ask, and wait for her to dig them from the bottom of her bag.

Even breaking in, hot-wiring would take longer than the additional burst of speed and extra twenty-five yards they'd need to reach his Benz.

"My car. Let's go," he ordered.

She followed, yelping once, cursing once, twice, yet sticking by his side all the way.

A shot cracked the pavement to the right of their path, a clean shot straight between two of the garage's support beams. Way too close for comfort.

Rivers's practice was about to make perfect in ways Julian didn't want to consider.

The keyless transponder in his pocket activated the entry into his car from three feet away. He touched the handle, jerked open the SL500's driver's side door.

Katrina scrambled across the console, tossed her bag onto the floor; he slid down into his seat, punched the ignition button, shoved the transmission into reverse.

Tires screaming, he whipped backwards out of the parking space and shot down the long row of cars. He hit the street ass-backwards, braked, spun, shifted into first, and floored it, high-octane adrenaline fueling his flight.

Halfway down Grand, several near misses and an equal number of traffic violations later, he cast a quick sideways glance at Katrina and nodded. "You might want to buckle up."

She cackled like she'd never heard anything more ridiculous. "You're suggesting that now?"

He shrugged, keeping an eye on his rearview and any unwanted company, whether Rivers or the cops. He wasn't about to stop for either. "Better late than never."

That earned him a snort, but she did as she'd been told. Then she lifted her left foot into her lap, giving him an eyeful of a whole lotta tanned and toned thigh. "I've got glass in my foot."

He didn't say anything. He had to get out of her neighborhood and ditch his car—a reality that seriously grated. "Stitches?"

She shook her head, leaning down for a closer look at the damage. "I don't think so. Tweezers, antibiotic ointment, and a bandage should suffice."

"I've got a first aid kit in the trunk." How many times had he patched himself up on the fly? "I'll grab it as soon as we stop. In the meantime . . ." He pulled his handkerchief from his pocket.

"Thanks." She halved it into a triangle and wrapped her foot securely, knotting the fabric on top at the base of her toes. "When you hit 95, head south. The police station's on Sunset."

He nodded, turned north at the next intersection.

"Uh, hello? I said Sunset. South, not north."

"I heard you." This wasn't the time for a long explanation as to why he couldn't go to the police, why SG-5 couldn't risk exposure, why he'd learned a long time ago that actions spoke a hell of a lot louder than words.

"Look," she said, settling her sunglasses that he happened to know were Kate Spade firmly in place. "I appreciate the save, even if I was dumb as a stick to get in this car not knowing who you are. But we're going to the police, or I'll be making a scene like you wouldn't believe."

Oh, he believed Miss High Maintenance capable of just that. So far the only surprise had been her lack of complaints over their full out hundred-yard dash and the injury she'd sustained in the process.

"This isn't a police matter." Still, heading in the direction of the station might keep Rivers at bay and give Julian time to consider his options.

"And why would that be?" she asked, her incredulous tone of voice unable to mask the sound of the gears whirring in her mind. "You're with the shooter, aren't you? This kidnapping was the goal all along. You sonofabitch."

Julian couldn't help it. He smiled. It was something he rarely did for good reason, and the twitch of unused facial muscles felt strange.

But there was just something about a woman with a sailor's mouth that grabbed hold of his gut and twisted him up with the possibilities.

He hadn't had a really good mouth in a very long time.

A thought that sobered him right up. "No. I'm not with the shooter. His name is Benny Rivers. He's with Spectra IT and he's in Miami to take you out."

And here's a peek at

THE McKENZIE ARTIFACT

The drapes over his motel room's window pulled open, Eli McKenzie stood and stared through the mottled glass, squinting at the starburst shards of sunlight reflected off the windshields of the cars barreling down Highway 90 in the distance.

Second floor up meant he could see Del Rio, Texas, on the horizon, and to his left a silvery sliver of the twisting Rio Grande, a snake reminding him of the venom he'd be facing once he harnessed the guts to cross.

The room's cooling unit blew tepid air up his bare torso, making a weak attempt at drying the persistent sheet of sweat. Sweat having less to do with the heat of the day than with the choking memory of the poison he'd unknowingly ingested on his last trip here.

An accidental ingestion. A purposeful poisoning.

Someone in Mexico wanted him dead.

The only surprise there was that no one but Rabbit knew Eli's true identity. Wanting to dispose of an SG-5 operative was one thing, but he hadn't been made. Which meant this was personal.

This was about his covert identity, his posing as a member of the Spectra IT security team guarding the compound across the border.

An identity he'd lived and breathed for six months until the nausea and dysarthria, the diarrhea, ataxia and tremors turned him into a monster. One everyone around him wanted to kill.

He'd tried himself. Once.

Rabbit had stopped him and sent him back to New York and to Hank Smithson, the Smithson Group principal, to heal. Eli owed both men his life, though it was his debt to Hank that weighed heaviest.

Hank, who plucked men in need of redemption off their personal highways to hell and set them down on roads less traveled. Roads that took the SG-5 operatives places not a one of them wished to see again after reaching the end of their missions.

Places like the Spectra IT compound in Mexico.

Scratching the center of his chest, Eli shook his head and pondered his immediate future. He and Rabbit were the only ones inside the compound not working for Spectra. Outside was a different story.

And there had been one person nosing around and causing enough scenes to make a movie.

Stella Banks.

Stella Banks with her platinum blonde hair and battered straw cowboy hat and legs longer than split rail fence posts. She was an enigma. A private investigator who dressed like a barrel racer and looked like a runway model.

She kept an office in Ciudad Acuna, another in Del Rio. He knew she was working the disappearance of her office manager's daughter, Carmen Garcia. The girl was fourteen, and like so many of the others gone missing recently, a beauty.

She was also currently being held inside the compound,

waiting to be shipped away from her family and into a life of prostitution courtesy of Spectra IT. Or so had been the case last Eli had checked in with Rabbit.

The room wasn't getting any cooler, the day any longer, the truth of what lay ahead any easier to swallow. Like it or not, it was time to go. Once across the border, he'd make his way south a hundred kilometers in the heap Rabbit had left parked in a field west of the city.

As much as Eli longed for a haircut and a shave, he wouldn't bother with either. The scruffy disguise went a long way to helping him blend in, to hiding the disgust he never quite wiped from his face.

Considering the condition of the car and the roads, he was looking at a good two hours of travel time. One hundred and twenty minutes to go over the plans he'd worked out with Rabbit to take down these bastards.

Plans trickier than Eli liked to deal with but which couldn't be helped. Not with the lives of twenty teenaged girls on the line.

He hadn't quite nailed down his plans for Stella Banks.

He needed her out of the way.

Before he got rid of her, however, he needed to find out what she and her outside sources could add to what Rabbit had learned on the inside.

Only then would Eli make certain she never interfered in his mission again.

He was alive.

And he was back.

That son-of-a-bitch was back.

Stella Banks curled her fingers through the chain links of the fenced enclosure and watched him leave the compound's security office and cross the yard to the barracks.

She couldn't believe it. Not after all the trouble she'd gone through—and gotten into—to get rid of his sorry kidnapping ass for good.

Next time she'd forgo the poison and use a bullet instead.